STUART MCHARDY has lectured and written on many aspects of Scottish history and folklore both in Scotland and abroad. His life-long interest in all aspects of Scottish culture led to his becoming a founding member and president of the Pictish Arts Society. From 1993-98 he was also the Director of the Scots Language Resource Centre in Perth. Following many years on the seminal 'McGregor's Gathering' (BBC Radio Scotland) he has continued to broadcast on radio and television. He lectures annually at Edinburgh University's Centre for Continuing Education in the areas of Scottish mythology, folklore and legend. He is also the author of a children's book, *The Wild Haggis and the Greetin-faced Nyaff* (Scottish Children's Press, 1995) and has had poetry in Scots and English published in many magazines. Born in Dundee, McHardy is a graduate of Edinburgh University and lives in that city today with his wife Sandra.

Luath Storyteller Series
Tales of the Picts

STUART McHARDY

Luath Press Limited

EDINBURGH

www.luath.co.uk

First published 2005

The paper used in this book is recyclable. It is made
from low chlorine pulps produced in a low energy,
low emission manner from renewable forests.

The publisher acknowledges subsidy from

 Scottish
Arts Council

towards the publication of this book.

Printed and bound by
Bookmarque Ltd., Croydon

Typeset in 10 point Sabon by
S. Fairgrieve, Edinburgh

For all those who know themselves to be latter-day Picts.

contents

Introduction

TO THE NORTH of Dundee stands a broken Pictish Symbol Stone called Martin's Stane. There is a story of nine maidens associated with this stone that links it to other stories in many divergent cultures over millennia. As a lad of seven and eight years old I used to pass this stone on my way to walk through the nearby hills, the Sidlaws – 'Seedlies' in the local dialect – whose name is generally translated as the Fairy Hills. Even in primary school I was fascinated by the ancient peoples of Scotland and was lucky enough to have a history teacher in secondary school who encouraged this interest, D B Taylor. On bus trips round hill-forts, stone circles and other ancient monuments, I began to develop a particular interest in the people we call the Picts.

These were the people who saw off the Romans and left a magnificent corpus of carved Symbol Stones throughout eastern and northern Scotland: one of the great artistic treasures of mankind. The influence of Pictish art on such weel-kent treasures as the Books of Kells and Durrow was seminal, and is only now beginning to be truly understood. Much of the metalwork generally called Insular Celtic is in fact Pictish, and there has been an abundance of work in Scotland over the centuries derived from the magnificent artistic

traditions of this ancient tribal people. My lifelong
fascination with the Picts, who in the oral tradition
of the people of much of Scotland are effectively
'the ancestor people', led me to the stories that
have been, and still are being, told about them.
The stories are often associated with particular
stones or locales but some, like the story of the
Heather Yill, crop up in many places. For many
years these stories have been running around my
head and in my role as a storyteller I have told
many of them again and again.

These stories speak to me in a way that others
do not, perhaps because I think of myself as a
direct descendant of the Picts, even though in truly
Scottish fashion I have Scandinavian and Irish
blood in my veins – making me just one more of
Jock Tamson's mongrel bairns. Whether standing
in a museum looking at one of the great Cross
slabs of the later Christian Picts, or out in some
field looking at the simple, elegant and expressive
picked-out symbols of the earlier pagan Picts,
I have a sense of continuity and belonging that
brings a glow of pleasure. Likewise the stories
have always touched a nerve. History is always
corrupted by propaganda – implicitly or
explicitly. The tales that survive in oral tradition,
unconcerned with provable fact or specific historical
individuals, speak to us in a different way than the
historians' attempts to give us a clear, structured

vision of the past. Story is concerned with human truth, not observable data, and has no need to pretend to precision in factual terms. It is part of the continuity of all oral traditions that stories will over time change to suit their audience – it is as if they change their clothes to suit changing environments and they continue to be told as long as they have relevance for the teller and the audience.

Though we have almost no written material from the Picts themselves we must remember that story can tell us much. While history is concerned with dates and places, and the furtherance of the interests of those who paid for it to be written, story has a different agenda. Stories can be told for thousands of years and hold on to real data about actual events, but they survive because they matter to those who hear them as much as to those who tell them. Some of these tales might be very old indeed, some might be about actual historical events while others seem to have arisen as attempts to explain the strange symbols so lovingly carved by the Picts. Many of them undoubtedly come from a time before most people could read or write, and were part of the cultural treasure of their times, as they are now part of ours.

The stories here have changed their clothes more than most, in that they are my creative re-working of material that has come down through the traditions of my ancestors over hundreds and hundreds of years. Some of the stories I have heard from other storytellers, others have been found as scraps of tradition in old books. All of them stem from the time when the people of Scotland thought of the Picts, more properly the Pechts, as their ancestors, and there can be little doubt that some of them retain material that has survived from the time of the Picts themselves. I have been called a latter-day Pict (and worse) because of my deep interest in this ancient tribal people, which led to the setting up of the Pictish Arts Society* with a group of like-minded friends.

To this day debate rages over the meaning, or meanings of the Pictish Symbols and the more we study them the more likely we will, in time, understand them. In the aftermath of the setting up of Scotland's Parliament it is time to try and develop a clearer understanding of Scotland's history in all its aspects and in presenting these stories I hope I can stimulate others to find inspiration in that common history.

Stuart McHardy
June 2005

* For more information, contact the Pictish Arts Society, c/o Pictavia, Haughmuir, by Brechin, DD9 6RL.
www.pictarts.demon.co.uk

general tales

the piper of pict's knowe

N O MATTER WHAT historians and scholars say, people all over Scotland thought that the Picts were their ancestors. Even in the Border country there are stories relating back to them. One of these was a tale from Ednam, a wee village not far from Kelso, within the lands of the ancient Gododdin, whom the Romans called the Votadini. Just half a mile or so west of the village is an old burial mound, and like many such tumuli across Scotland it has its own tale. It was a place that the local people kept away from, especially after dark for there were often strange lights to be seen and eerie music would be heard. This, it was said, was the Picts, living in that strange half-world between the natural and supernatural. Just like the fairies they were said to be exceedingly fond of music and dancing. But it was believed that if you got too close you would become enchanted by the marvellous strains of their songs and tunes and be spirited away to the other side and never be seen again. Many instances were told of people who had stayed too close to the Pict's Knowe after darkness fell, and were gone by morning, and such disappearances were the subject of regular discussion in the tavern in Ednam village.

At one time there was a piper in Ednam, when

it was common for towns to have official pipers. Now Ednam was maybe a bit too wee to have its own official full time piper but the piper it had, by the name of Willie Holton, still managed to make a fair enough living playing for weddings, dances and funerals, and the odd nights in the taverns round about. When he played in the taverns of course he used the bellows-pipes, for long so popular over the country, for the sound of the great bagpipe in a room whose ceiling was no more than six foot high would do more than get the feet tapping – it would likely to get the ears bleeding too! Now Willie lived in Ednam itself and whenever there was no work to be found in the surrounding countryside he would head for the tavern in the middle of the village where people were usually happy to at least buy him a drink or two if he played a few tunes. And like one or two other pipers, and other musicians down the years, or so I have heard tell, he might sometimes have a drink or two too many.

One night he had been playing for a few hours and had stopped for a break. He was sitting sipping his ale with a couple of locals when the talk came round to the Pict's Knowe.

'Aye, my every own great-grandfather was stolen awa by the picts in yon knowe, it's an oorie place, even in the daytime,' said Tam Soutar, a big florid-faced man who had a farm just a couple of miles to the west of the village.

'Aye, I'd heard that,' put in Johnny Wilson, the local carter. 'You'd never get me oot there after dark, never.'

'Aye, aye,' Willie interjected, 'but I've heard it said by mony anither piper that some o' the tunes the Picts play are fine indeed.'

'Wheesht, Willie,' Soutar said, looking around him. 'Dinnae even think such things, it's the magic in that music that stole my great-grandfather away, thon stuff is no for human ears.'

'Well, maybe aye,' mused Willie, taking a mouthful of beer, 'but maybe no. I'm sure that if a man was careful enough he could get close in to the Knowe and listen to the music. I've a pretty good ear for a tune and I doubt it would nae take me long tae catch one o' their songs.'

His two companions were aghast and pleaded with the piper not to even consider such a dangerous course of action. They had no doubt what the outcome of such stupidity would be, and as they were both good friends of the piper, they persuaded him that it would be a daft idea indeed. Or so they thought.

Once Willie said he wouldn't go and try to steal one of the Picts' tunes, his pals relaxed. Another round of drinks was bought and Willie struck up a set of brisk reels that soon had the whole tavern tapping their feet. But then closing time came round and all there said good night to one another and headed home, some alone, others in twos and threes. Willie went back towards his house with the carter, who lived a bit further on, but once Johnny had said good night and walked off, he quickly turned back and made his way west through the village. The idea of a magic Pictish tune that only he could play had been running through his mind all night. With such a tune he could become the best-known piper in all the Borders. He would be famous and he would likely be pretty well off too.

These thoughts were whirling through his mind as he headed over the fields towards the Pict's Knowe. As he passed through the end of the village he was seen by the Widow Haxton who was putting in her cat, but he didn't even notice her.

She was the very last human in Ednam to lay eyes on Willie Holton. The following day there was no sign of him, but as he was prone to wandering the countryside no one paid much attention to his absence. Three days later however, there was a wedding arranged and when the bride's father knocked on Willie's door there was no answer. He went to the tavern and asked if anyone had seen the piper. No one there had seen him for a couple of days. Well, villages are pretty much the same everywhere and within an hour or two everybody had heard that the last that had been seen of Willie Holton the piper was the night he had headed west, towards the fateful mound.

It was with a heavy heart and a chilling sense
of foreboding that Tam Soutar, Johnny Wilson and
a small group of other local men went out to the
Pict's Knowe at noon the following day. There
lying on the top of the ancient tumulus were Willie
Holton's bellows-pipes, the ones he'd been carrying
when last seen. But of Willie himself there was not
a trace, then or ever again. And it was in sadness
for their departed musician that the local people
changed the name of that strange and dangerous
place from the Pict's Knowe to the Piper's Knowe.
And there was many a night in the Ednam tavern
that his friends toasted the piper hoping maybe
that he was managing to play a few tunes for the
Picts who had spirited him away.

aBeRnethy toweR

SCOTLAND HAS ONLY two of the peculiar high towers
that are so often associated with early monasteries
in Ireland and one of them is at Abernethy – an
important Christian centre long before the creation
of St Andrews. The other one is at Brechin, another
Christian centre highly important in the time of the
Picts. These towers are over twenty metres tall and,
apart from the door, they have no openings in their
walls, leading many people to think that they were
primarily used for defensive purposes. One suggestion
has been that the monks would run and hide in

these towers whenever raiders approached, and we know that for much of the first millennium there were plenty of raiders about!

Whatever they were for, the people of Abernethy know who built their tower: the Picts, a fearsomely strong people who handled great blocks of stone as if they were little more than pebbles. By the time they built Abernethy tower they had become nocturnal and were never seen about in the day by the other peoples of early Scotland. Whether this was because they were frightened of the light or just preferred the dark has never been found out, but they went out of their way to try never to be seen.

When, for reasons of their own, they decided to build Abernethy Tower, they went at it in a strange fashion. A whole tribe of them stood in a long line from their great quarry at Drimdreill in the Lomond Hills all the way north to Abernethy, up hillsides and down, standing in rivers and burns when necessary.

Starting just after nightfall they passed the great blocks of quarried stone from hand to hand all the way from the Lomonds to Abernethy, near the banks of the Tay. Here they began to build and as the night passed the great tower began to rise over Abernethy. Throughout the night they laboured and slowly the tower grew in height. At last it was tall enough for them to finish it off and they were ready to raise a spire on top of the tower. But their excitement became too great and they carried on working even as the sun rose over the world. Just at the dawn, an old woman rose from her bed and came to the door of her simple house to empty her potty and saw them. She let out a cry of surprise and terror, for she had long heard that the Picts were a wild and dangerous lot. This upset the Picts so much they fled off into the hills, leaving the tower unfinished, which is why the Abernethy tower has no spire to this day!

heather yill

AMONGST THEIR CONTEMPORARIES; the Scots, Britons and – in later years – the Norsemen, the Picts were particularly envied for one thing. It wasn't their great strength or their remarkable stamina, both of which made them fearsome enemies. What the other peoples wanted for themselves was the recipe for heather yill, the strong sweet alcoholic drink that the Picts, versed in ancient herbal lore, made from the tops of the heather plant. Given the amount of heather that grows in Scotland, the advantages of being able to make drink from it were obvious. Heather was something no one would ever run out of! However the Picts, though happy enough to trade their yill for other goods – and usually exacting a high price – were absolutely firm in their refusal to hand over the recipe. The leader or chief of each community or tribe of the Picts was the one who had the knowledge and this was passed from father to son. Sons were always given the secret so if the father fell in battle someone would be able to carry on the tradition.

Once, a chief of one of the Scottish tribes went on a raid to Galloway with the specific aim of getting the secret, and one after another kidnapped a number of Pictish warriors. All of them were tortured extensively but not one of them would say a word about the heather yill. The Scots didn't know that only the chiefs and their sons had the secret and all of the Pictish warriors went to their deaths before giving up even that knowledge!

The frustration of the Scots increased but one day they had the good fortune, they thought, to come upon the chief of the Picts and his son near a cliff-top on the Rhinns of Galloway. There was no escape. Behind the elderly Pict and his son there was only the sea, and before them twenty odd heavily armed Scots warriors.

'Surrender or die,' called the leader of the Scots, and the old Pict put down his spear, as did his son.

'Now,' said the Scottish chief, 'we want to know the secret of the heather yill. If you don't tell us we will kill you both, and we'll take our time in doing it!'

'Well,' said the Pictish chief, 'before I tell ye, ye'll have to do something for me.'

'And what's that?' asked the Scot suspiciously.

'Well, ye see it would shame me to give away the secrets of my ancestors in front of my son here. So ye'll have to kill him.'

'WHAT?' gasped the Scot, as the young Pict looked at his father with terror in his eyes, his mouth open in disbelief.

'Aye, aye, that's the way it has to be,' said the old grey-haired Pict, slowly shaking his head and looking sadly at his son.

The Scottish chief took him at his word and before the younger Pict had really understood what was happening he was lying dead at his father's feet.

'Now then,' said the Scot, 'what about it?'

'What about what?' answered the Pict.

'This heather yill, the recipe – that's what,' rasped the Scot. 'You said you'd tell us once your son was dead. He's lying there like a log at your feet, now give us the recipe.'

'Och aye,' said the Pict slowly, 'so I did. And you believed me?'

'Aye, we believed you,' replied the Scot, 'that's why we killed your laddie.'

'Ach well,' said the Pict with a wee smile, 'ye might as well kill me too, for I'll never tell you how to brew the heather yill.'

And so they did.

stevenson poem

ROBERT LOUIS STEVENSON, one of Scotland's greatest writers, had his own version of the heather ale story, which he put into a poem.

Heather Ale
A Galloway Legend

From the bonny bells of heather
They brewed a drink long-syne,
Was sweeter far than honey,
Was stronger far than wine.
They brewed it and they drank it,
And lay in a blessed swound
For days and days together
In their dwellings underground.

There rose a king in Scotland,
A fell man to his foes,
He smote the Picts in battle,
He hunted them like roes.
Over miles of the red mountain
He hunted as they fled,
And strewed the dwarfish bodies
Of the dying and the dead.

Summer came in the country,
Red was the heather bell;
But the manner of the brewing
Was none alive to tell.
In graves that were like children's
On many a mountain head,
The Brewsters of the Heather
Lay numbered with the dead

The king in the red moorland
Rode on a summer's day;
And the bees hummed, and the curlews
Cried beside the way.
The king rode, and was angry,
Black was his brow and pale,
To rule in a land of heather
And lack the Heather Ale.

It fortuned that his vassals,
Riding free on the heath,
Came on a stone that was fallen
And vermin hid beneath.
Rudely plucked from their hiding,
Never a word they spoke:
A son and his aged father –
Last of the dwarfish folk.

The king sat high on his charger,
He looked on the little men;
And the dwarfish and swarthy couple
Looked at the king again.
Down by the shore he had them;
And there on the giddy brink –
'I will give you life, ye vermin,
For the secret of the drink.'

There stood the son and father
And they looked high and low;
The heather was red around them,
The sea rumbled below.
And up and spoke the father,
Shrill was his voice to hear:
'I have a word in private,
A word for the royal ear.

Life is dear to the aged,
And honour a little thing;
I would gladly sell the secret,'
Quoth the Pict to the King.
His voice was small as a sparrow's,
And shrill and wonderful clear:
'I would gladly sell my secret,
Only my son I fear.

For life is a little matter,
And death is nought to the young;
And I dare not sell my honour
Under the eye of my son.
Take him, O king, and bind him,
And cast him far in the deep;
And it's I will tell the secret
That I have sworn to keep.'

They took the son and bound him,
Neck and heels in a thong,
And a lad took him and swung him,
And flung him far and strong,
And the sea swallowed his body,
Like that of a child of ten; —
And there on the cliff stood the father,
Last of the dwarfish men.

'True was the word I told you:
Only my son I feared;
For I doubt the sapling courage
That goes without the beard.
But now in vain is the torture,
Fire shall never avail:
Here dies in my bosom
The secret of Heather Ale.'

R L stevenson's father meets a pict

THE IDEA OF the Picts being their ancestors held a remarkable grip on people's imaginations. When we remember that almost universal literacy is only a century or so old in Scotland, and that only two or three generations ago most people travelled rarely and not very far, it is easy to understand how ancient stories could retain a strong hold on people's minds. This tenacity of belief was shown remarkably in Orkney a hundred and fifty years ago.

There, like many places in Scotland, people believed that the Picts were wee, dark and exceedingly hairy people, who haunted the ancient ruins and wild places of the countryside, keeping out of sight of decent people. Now, one time Robert Louis Stevenson's father Thomas was in Orkney surveying the coast for a new lighthouse, and he had a startling encounter with belief in the Picts. He was one of a remarkable family who for several generations built all the lighthouses and many harbours all round Scotland's coasts. Many of these showed great skill in their construction, since some buildings were being built on rocks that were only above the level of the sea for a few hours a day. For centuries Scottish shipping had been a dangerous business and the contribution of the Stevenson family to saving the lives of Scotland's sailors, and the profits of the ship-owners, is one that can never be overstated.

This particular time Thomas Stevenson and a colleague were visited in their lodgings by a distraught local. He begged them to come with him and help him and his neighbours with a desperate problem. Their help was sought because they were educated men and whatever the problem was it was taxing the powers of the local community. The local told them that a Pict had turned up in their village. This was met with utter disbelief by Stevenson and his friend, both of whom were exhausted after a hard day's work scouring the rocky coastline, but the local was insistent. They had found a Pict in their village and they needed help. The creature was a wee dark, hairy man with great big feet, clad in strange shaped shoes, dressed in rags, and he couldn't speak. He had come into the village and collapsed.

The engineers were hardly keen to go outside, it was a wild night and they were comfortable by the fire. However the man was in such a state of distress they thought they should try to help and at last agreed to go. When they reached the nearby village they were ushered into a humble cottage, which was surrounded by a crowd even in the biting cold. Inside yet more people were grouped around a bed on which lay the Pict. The mood of the people was sombre and mutterings of 'get rid of it' and other such comments could be heard. In truth the man sound asleep on the bed was very small, not much over four feet and had a mass of unkempt hair and a big black beard. His clothes were stitched together rags and his feet were encased in extremely crude boots, obviously hand-made by someone with little if any cobbling skill.

It seems Stevenson might have had trouble keeping a straight face for he in fact recognised the sleeping Pict. He was a man who had been a shop-keeper in Edinburgh until one day he got the call to go on the road and spread the word of the Lord. He had given away all his worldly goods and left the city to wander wherever his feet took him, spreading the Gospel and living as simply as he could. He had eventually ended up in Orkney, got lost, and by the time he found the village was in a state of absolute exhaustion, made worse by not having eaten for several days, if not longer. His life on the road accounted for his appearance – he had ended up making his own boots, with no skill or instruction in that particular art.

The villagers took some convincing but when the Pict at last opened his eyes, recognised Stevenson and spoke to him in Scots, their scepticism disap-peared. Their fears that an ancient Pict had burst forth from a burial mound to wreak havoc among them could be laid to rest.

the pict's song

IN THE OLDEN times most people lived out in the countryside and had to grow their own food. Much of the trading that went on was exchange of goods, or bartering, and even the rich folk in their big houses grew their own food, or rather had it grown for them in their extensive gardens. In the towns there were food shops but out in the country people couldn't even buy flour to bake bread. They had to grow the wheat or corn to make it. This is why oatcakes are so much a part of traditional Scottish fare, as oats will grow any-where in Scotland. So people would have to take the grain they had grown themselves to local mills to be ground into flour, which they would then use to make bread or bannocks, the traditional Scottish flat cakes made from oats or barley.

For long enough in old Scotland the diet of the people revolved mainly around barley and oats, with a few root vegetables and some meat and dairy products. Each area had to have its own mill, and often people were obliged to use the one owned by their landlord. The miller was a central figure in most communities and the mill itself was an absolutely essential community resource, one which generally turned out to be profitable for the owner. Sometimes mills were operated directly by the smallholders or crofters who occupied most of

Lowland Scotland till the eighteenth century, and it was common that their rent would include a charge for the privilege of having the mill. The rents of course were generally paid in kind, with food or other products produced on the crofts, as there was very little money about.

On the eastern side of the Shetland island of Fetlar there was a mill known as Fir Vaa – a water mill. One night Gilbert Lawrenson, who lived nearby, took his corn to the mill to grind it. He carried the great, heavy sack on his back and was relieved to get to the mill. He reckoned he could get some sleep while his corn was being ground. Emptying the corn into the hopper, he set the mill in motion and went off for a rest. Just beside the mill there was a wee house, little more than a shed really, where people could wait while the corn was ground. It was a pretty basic building, four walls and a roof, no fireplace and just a pile of straw to sit on. Still it provided shelter from the wind, which as any Shetlander will tell you, can get pretty wild on the islands.

This was at the time when snuff was very popular and once Gilbert sat himself down he had a snort or two of snuff and snuggled into the straw. He wasn't quite asleep, just nodding away at the edge of sleep in a state a bit like daydreaming. At first he thought he really was dreaming for he began to hear music, coming from outside by the mill. The music got a bit louder and suddenly

Gilbert was fully awake. He knew, somehow, what was happening.

Now at this time the Picts, the wee dark folk, were still about on the islands and they had a habit of stealing people's boats whenever they needed to journey between the islands. Fir Vaa was right down near the shore and Gilbert suspected that the peerie, or little fowk, as they were called locally, were coming into land in a boat they had stolen. The Picts would take one and just leave it wherever suited them and many a boat had been left to drift off to sea. They were believed to have been forced into hiding by the coming of the big people, the current Shetlanders, and generally only came out at night. Now the people needed their boats to catch fish to eat, and maybe sometimes, if they were lucky, sell to passing ships. The Picts' stealing of the boats was considered a real nuisance by the islanders. Gilbert was fully awake now and heard the Picts land on the beach and the music got even louder. It sounded as if they were coming straight towards the wee house by the mill! Gilbert didn't know what to do so he buried himself as deep as he could in the pile of straw he had been lying on, and pretended to be asleep.

In came the Picts and saw him lying there. One or two of them wanted to play tricks on him but one of them just said. 'Ach let him be, I've seen this one about the place, he's all right. Let him sleep.'

All this time the music carried on and Gilbert opened his eyes – just a wee crack – to see what was going on.

'Come on let's have another tune now boy,' said one of the wee dark men just out of Gilbert's sight. Slowly, so as not to give the game away, he moved as if in his sleep, till he could see the musician. It was a tiny wee dark man with a porsh – an ancient one-stringed fiddle the Picts liked to play, and the wee fellow certainly could play it. As he played a lively, spirited tune with great gusto all the other Picts started to dance. Round and round they went as the musician played like the Devil himself. They were all caught up in the music and paid no attention to Gilbert lying there in the straw. On and on the music went, right through the night and on to the morning. Gilbert felt as if he was caught in a dream as he listened to the tune repeated time and again through the hours of darkness.

Then, as the sun came up, the music came to an abrupt end. The Picts stopped their dancing and without a word they all went out of the wee house. Gilbert lay still till he heard their footsteps fade as they headed into the hinterland of the island, where they were thought to live in underground houses like their ancestors of old. It was widely believed that the Picts had considerable magic powers and people were keen to avoid them if at all possible.

Only when he was sure that the Picts were well

away did Gilbert think to move. He quickly went to the mill to get his flour. He filled his sack and as he did so he kept humming the tune the wee Pict had been playing most of the night on his porsh. Once he had his flour, he hoisted the big sack on his back again and set off home, all the time humming and whistling the Pictish tune. He thought he would come back and have a look at the boat the Picts had landed in later on.

Now Gilbert had a pretty good ear for a tune but he was not much use on the fiddle. His son though, wee Gibbie, was turning out to be a very fine fiddler indeed. So as soon as he got home, without explaining where he had been all night to his stern-faced wife, he told his son to fetch his fiddle, and once he had done that Gilbert whistled the tune to him. Once, twice and then a third time he whistled the tune and wee Gibbie, caught up in his father's excitement, dashed it off on the fiddle, almost note perfect. A few wee changes were all that was necessary and the boy had the tune. Only then did Gilbert turn to his wife, 'I was caught up in the wee hoose at the mill, lass. In came a bunch o' Picts and they played their fiddle and danced all night. That's the tune they were playin that wee Gibbie has just learned,' and he stood there smiling.

His wife was relieved at the news, even if she was a bit frightened by the thought that he had been all night in the same house as a bunch of

Picts, for she knew well, as did everyone, that they could be right bad and spiteful wee creatures. But her man was safe, so it was all right and she had to admit that the tune was a fine one. Gilbert himself was pleased that he had got one over on the Picts by stealing one of their tunes, and when word got round everybody wanted to hear Wee Gibbie play it.

And that is how the tune they call *Winyadepla* became part of the Shetland repertoire. The name was taken from the wee lochan above the Lawrensons' croft, though wee Gibbie always called it *Old Gibbie's Tune* in honour of his father.

NORRIE'S LAW

ON THE NORTH side of the river Forth stands Largo Law, overlooking the coastal village of Upper Largo. A mile beyond the Law is the remains of an ancient burial mound, known locally as Norrie's Law, which is linked to Largo Law by a strange tale. On the slopes of Largo Law itself the children would play a widely known game, but with its own local slant. One child would stand in front of a group of pals and say,

'A'll tell ye a story
Aboot Tammie o' Norrie
If ye dinnae speak in the middle o' it
Will ye no?'

The idea was simple, to make one of the other, probably younger, children say no, and thus the story couldn't be told. This is a very widespread bairn's game, the difference here being the mention of Tammie o' Norrie, a local cowherd who figures in the tale.

There was a local tradition that a ghost haunted the slopes of Largo Law; a ghost of a robber that was condemned to roam the earth till it could unburden itself of a secret. The secret was where the ghost had buried his gold. In life he had been an evil creature driven by the lust for gold and in death his obsession cursed him. He had no hope of attaining eternal bliss unless he could tell his secret. Many people had thought to help the poor creature by listening to his tale, and of course get some benefit for themselves for their kindness. But all – when confronted by the grim apparition in the gloaming on the shores of the Law – had been unable to control their terror and had run away.

Eventually though, one local man, a shepherd on the farm of Balmain, decided that he was just the man to approach the ghost and relieve it of its burden, thereby enriching himself. Like the robber he was driven by dreams of wealth and was a sour and bitter man, dissatisfied with his lot as a shepherd. He thought he deserved better and if he could get the buried treasure the people of the area would see his true mettle! He thought about it long and hard and then one evening, summoning up all his courage he went to Largo Law in the gloaming, hoping to

meet the unfortunate spirit. Walking along the
northern shoulder of the hill in the darkening light
he saw what appeared to be a shimmering cloud of
smoke not far in front of him. As he watched the
strange shimmering it seemed to solidify and in the
blink of an eye he found himself confronted by the
ghost. A tall deathly-looking figure it was. The spectre
looked long at him, causing his blood to run cold,
and stood silent before him.

'I have come . . .' he stammered, and fell silent,
flinching under the steely gaze of the undead eyes.
He steeled himself and spoke again. 'I have come to
listen to your tale and help you seek eternal rest.'

The creature looked long and hard at him and
it seemed as if a cold vice had grabbed his heart.
Then a sepulchral voice boomed out:

'If Auchendowrie cock disnae craw,
An' the herd o Balmain disnae blaw,
A'll tell ye where the gowd is on Largo Law.
Come here on the morrow an dinnae be late
For I'll no wait longer than the hour o' eight.'

At that the spirit shimmered and seemed to drift
away like smoke on the soft breeze blowing off the
river. The shepherd was shaking with excitement.
He was going to be rich! The next day at eight o'
clock he would know where the buried treasure was.
All he had to do was follow the ghost's instructions.
What had he said? 'If Auchendowrie cock disnae
craw' – that was easily enough done, he thought.

The other bit, 'An' the herd o Balmain disnae blaw' – well, he could sort that too. The cowherd of Balmain was Tammie o' Norrie, a man he had little time or respect for, and he was sure he could stop him blowing on his horn to summon the cattle into the byre in the early evening without too much bother.

The following morning the entire household of Auchendowrie farm slept in. No cock had cried to waken the maid to light the fire. When the farmer's wife heard this and went to check she found her prize rooster dead on the dung heap, strangled. The shepherd had been round before dawn and later was waiting to catch Tammie o' Norrie as he took his cows out to pasture. He was standing leaning on a gatepost when Tammie drove the cattle out of the byre and through the farmyard.

'Hey you, Tammie o' Norrie, I want a word wi ye,' he said, looking furtively around.

Now Tammie knew who the shepherd was and was aware there were few people who had a good word to say about him but, never one to pay attention to gossip, he had nothing against the man.

'Aye, well whit is it?' Tammie asked, 'Be quick though, I've tae get these beasts out tae the pasture.'

'Listen tae me. Tonight ye had better no blaw yer horn tae summon the cows hame or it'll be the worse for ye, understand,' and he drew back his coat to reveal a long knife stuck in his belt.

'Whit dae ye mean? No blaw my horn? How

will I get the cattle hame?' Tammie asked, puzzled by this turn of events.

'Ye can run them in wi yer dugs,' snarled the shepherd, his hand clasping the handle of the knife, and glowering at Tammie. 'Mind what I say or ye'll suffer for it!' Saying that, he turned and stamped off.

Now Tammie was quite bemused by this. The man obviously was dangerous and had made it pretty clear what he wanted. However, Tammie was never a man that liked to be ordered about and as he looked after the retreating figure he muttered to himself, 'Aye well, we'll see, we'll see.'

That evening the shepherd made his way to the northern slope of the hill just before eight o' clock. Just as the wraith appeared and was about to speak, the sound of a cow horn floated through the air from Balmain. The ghost, deprived of its release from earthly torment, spat out the words:

'Woe tae the man that blew that horn,
Fae oot o that spot he shall ne'er be borne!'

and disappeared. In a blind rage the shepherd ran to the north, the thought of killing the Balmain cowherd pulsing in his mind. By the time he got to the pasture, it was too late. There stood the figure of Tammie o' Norrie, horn at his lips – turned to stone. The local people tried to shift the unfortunate man, but some magical force prevented them and in desperation, and some fear, they heaped a great mound of earth over the unfortunate cowherd. This was given the name of Norrie's Law.

This story seems to be a degenerate version of an even older tale that said that inside the mound was the body of an ancient warrior called Norroway who had been buried astride his horse in a suit of silver armour! What we do know is that sometime in the 1830s a local cadger, or carter, was digging sand out of the hill for some building he was doing when he made a remarkable discovery. He found a hoard of treasure and over a few years he sold most of it to a silversmith in Cupar who melted it down and re-used it.

Eventually the cadger's conscience got the better of him and he handed over the few remnants he had to the widow of the local landowner, the recently deceased General Durham. She in turn donated the material to what was then the Museum of Antiquities, and the few magnificent remnants of the original Norrie's Law hoard can be seen in the new Museum of Scotland. There are just a few bits and pieces including a pair of pins with Pictish symbols, a couple of lozenge-shaped pieces that once might have been part of a corselet of mail, and pieces of a sword hilt, helmet and scabbard.

the wise women

A STORY SHAKESPEARE told was that of MacBeth, one time Mormaer of Moray, perhaps the last great Pictish area. In Scotland it has been said by some that MacBeth's wife, called Gruoch, was married before, not to Gillcomain, the previous Mormaer of Moray, but to Duncan, who MacBeth killed in battle. This sounds much like Haermdrude picking her own consort and conforms in no way at all to the portrayal by Shakespeare of a pair of ambitious murderers and traitors. But some things he maybe had a better grasp of.

Just north of Aviemore there is a lochan by the side of the railway track called Loch nan Carraigean, which translates as the 'loch of the stones'. Tradition tells us that there used to be a stone circle here, one of those monumental constructions of our ancient ancestors that they raised to watch the sun and moon and tell the passing of the seasons. All over Britain there are tales that say such places were once used by the Druids, but here at Loch nan Carraigean is a different tale. Handed down through untold generations, the story is that there were religious attendants at the stone on Granish Moor. But they were not Druids; they were not even men. Three sisters held sway here and were known, like so many female groupings in the old, old times, for great knowledge of healing and the wonderful skill of telling the future. And here the mistresses of the stones received regular visitors coming to ask of their fate. Of these, the most important were the Kings of the Picts, come after the ceremony of kingship and sovereignty had placed them far above their fellow men to ask what the future held. And who knows? Perhaps MacBeth himself, knowing of the ancient ways of his ancestors, did come here when he had defeated Duncan in battle and taken Gruoch as his bride, for now he was the King himself.

ðenoon law

ON THE NORTHERN slopes of the Sidlaw Hills, not far from the ancient royal seat of Glamis, is the hillfort of Denoon Law. It is a place that has a haunting atmosphere all its own, and when the local Picts came to build it they found they had a real problem. It is not in a commanding strategic location and the builders originally wanted to put it on a nearby hilltop. But unknown to them this particular hilltop was sacred to the fairies, and as everyone used to know it is always a bad idea to cross the People of Peace, as once they were called in Scotland. It seems that the Queen of the Fairies herself took great umbrage when work commenced on the building. Using her supernatural powers she called on a bunch of demons and as soon as night fell on the hilltop they arrived to do their work.

When the Picts came back the following morning not one stone was left upon another. The demons had scattered all the work done the previous day. Now the Picts were long known for being a hardy and even stubborn people, and were hardly likely to be put off by this. So they set to work with a will and by the end of the second day they had raised even more of the intended fort than they had the day before. But once again, as soon as night fell and the builders returned to their homes below, the demons fell upon their work and tore it apart.

The following morning it was a scene of utter devastation that met the Picts as they came to continue their work. But the Picts were nothing if not dedicated when it came to their buildings and, stopping the work just long enough to send for even more skilled and capable stone workers from elsewhere in Strathmore, they started building once again. This third time the building was even stronger than before and, maybe thinking that third time lucky was the way of things, the Picts once again left their labours as night fell. But better and stronger built though it was, this was nothing to the denizens of Hell that had been summoned by the Queen of Fairies and yet again they fell to their destructive work with glee.

Now the Picts, up till then, had been reluctant to face down the supernatural powers they clearly understood were behind all this rampant vandalism,

but now they knew they had a fight on their hands.
So once again they built their very best all through
the day, but this time they left behind a wise and
experienced warrior to watch over the work when
they left. He was a hero of a thousand battles and
had fought all sorts of strange creatures in his
wanderings around the country. He had no doubt
that he could see off whoever or whatever it was
that was wreaking this constant destruction.
So there he stood, sword and shield in hand, ready
for what was to come, whatever it might be.

Night had just fallen on the land when a strange
and powerful wind whipped up and whirled around
him. Earth and small stones were being lifted and
flung in his face, though he could clearly see that
beyond the environs of the hill, all was calm. But he
had no fear of magic and, covering his eyes behind
his shield, he peered around. A demon whipped past
in the air and he swung at it, but missed. Another
passed and he swung again with the same result.

'Still,' he thought to himself, 'if they are going
to spend their time tormenting me they will leave the
work alone and we can build on in the morning.'
So he gritted his teeth and lunged and poked at the
demons now filling the air around him. He was a
Pict. There were none braver and these foul fiends
were not enough to face him down!

But then came a noise. A noise much louder
even than the roaring wind. A noise that seemed to

fill the very heavens and shake the ground beneath his feet. And as his blood ran cold he realised it was a voice. A voice that dripped with venom as it boomed with such power his ears felt as if they were bleeding:

'Build not on this sacred ground,
It is sacred mongst the hills around.
Go build the castle on a bog,
Where it will neither shake nor shog.'

At that the voice rose to a piercing, blood-curdling shriek and the old warrior felt himself whipped up into the air and turned and tossed like leaf till he fell, apparently lifeless, at the foot of the hill.

Come the morning his companions found him barely alive, with just enough strength to tell them of the dreadful experience of the previous night, before he died. Up the hill they went and it was as if they had never been there. Even all the stones with which they had been building had disappeared! They knew now that they had to admit defeat. But what had the voice meant, 'build upon the bog?' Then one of them remembered. The hill we now know as Denoon Law was boggy on top. And so a bunch of saddened and chastened Picts buried their companion and set to draining the top of Denoon Hill and eventually built their fort there. And if you take the side off from the road to Glamis just before the village of Charlestown you will see it there yet.

the golden cradle

THE PICTS WERE on their last legs. Their King Druskin had fought long and bravely against the power of the Scots but his resistance was coming to an end. He knew fine well that the King of the Scots had too much support amongst the tribes and that his chances of living through the next battle were slim. Death was no disgrace for a warrior, but there was a deep and echoing sadness in his heart at the thought of the long line of Pictish rulers coming to an end. The Scots King, Kenneth the son of Alpine, had many Picts as well as Scots in his ranks. Some were the relations of his mother, a Pictish princess, while others thought he would be a better or more amenable king than Druskin. The King of the Picts, however, intended to show them all what he and his clan were made of. He had been forced back and back across Scotland till at last there was no place left to run to but the ancient capital of Abernethy, overlooking the Tay estuary. Here Pictish kings had ruled since time beyond memory and here he had been born himself. He had spent his first months in the Golden Cradle of the Picts, their most valuable treasure. It was one that the King of the Scots was desperate to take so his own descendants could sleep in it as bairns, preserving the ancient tradition and legitimising their rule over the Picts. It was a treasure that was generally believed to be magical and no one, not even the oldest and the wisest of the women, knew when it had been made.

But now Druskin had other things to think of than the practices of the past. He rallied his last troops to march out from the fort overlooking Abernethy to face the enemy, knowing that few if any of them would see another day. Behind him he left a small garrison of wounded warriors, old men and a few boys hardly tall enough to hold a spear. In ancient times the women would have been armed for battle too but he had told his wife and all his female relatives to make the best of what was to come. There was no need for them to follow their men to the Otherworld yet.

So Druskin marched out of the fort, banners streaming behind him as the keening of the women rose high on the wind blowing up from Strathearn and down the Tay estuary. The battle was fierce and the outcome just as expected. Druskin himself fell bravely at the front of his men and soon after that the Picts were routed. An advance guard of the Scots with Kenneth himself at their head made directly for Abernethy. Kenneth was sure that the remaining Picts would try to make off with the Cradle and Druskin's infant son inside it, in the hope of rallying in years to come. He was determined to take the fort with the Cradle and the infant still in it.

Within the fort the old men and wounded soldiers saw the approaching warriors, and many of them wanted to open the doors to the oncoming Scots king. Their army was defeated, there were only a few handfuls of them left, and what difference would it make for them to give up their lives in a futile last-ditch stand? Hadn't Druskin himself told the womenfolk to make the best of things? Well, shouldn't they too try to make the best of their situation?

As this discussion raged, Druskin's old nurse, who had charge of his infant son, went quietly to where the baby lay. 'These weak men have blood like water', she thought. They were not fit to call themselves Pictish warriors. Their king was doubtless dead out there on the battlefield and they were talking of surrendering to his killer? 'Cowards and traitors,' she spat as she lifted the Cradle with the sleeping infant in it. She might be old but she still had her health and she would show them how a true Pict should behave. Making her way to a secret door she let herself out on the side of the hill and headed upwards towards the lochan. Behind her she heard the Scots approaching the front of the fort. A fight broke out between those wanting to let the Scots in and those who were loyal to their oaths to defend the fort to the last. The upshot of this was that the Scots easily forced an entry and ran through the fort looking for the famous Golden Cradle and the Pictish king's baby son inside it.

It was nowhere to be found, but as Kenneth strode to the rampart of the fort he saw a figure up on the hill above – a figure carrying what looked like a golden cradle!

'Quick,' he cried, 'there's a woman heading up the hill with the Cradle! Get after her!'

At once a group of Scots streamed out of the fort and, running round its sides, headed up the hill. Amongst them were some of Kenneth's Pictish allies, eager to get the Cradle for themselves. By the time they reached the summit of the hill the nurse was standing on a large rock at the very edge of the deep, dark pool. As the men ran towards her she raised the Cradle above her head, gave a loud shriek and leapt into the lochan with the Cradle, and the king's son still inside! The dark waters of the lochan closed over her head just as King Kenneth arrived on the scene. At once he ordered some of his warriors to dive into the loch and retrieve the Cradle. They had barely time to lay down their weapons and undo the little armour they wore when the sky darkened. As if from nowhere great dark clouds whirled above them and a gale began to blow.

As they stood there, buffeted by the sudden wind and rain, the king turned to look at the centre of the lochan. There, rising slowly from the waters was an ancient, gigantic crone, haggard and wild-looking with dark skin and deep, piercing eyes.

The warriors all threw themselves to the ground at the sight of this supernatural female – all but the king. He stood rooted to the spot, unable to tear his eyes away from the gaze of this monstrous old carlin. A deep low sound, what initially he thought was just the wind, began to ring in his ears and he realised the carlin wife was speaking. No, she was chanting, in a deep, sepulchral voice that seemed to echo from the very edge of doom and was close to bursting the eardrums of all who heard her. And this is what the great carlin chanted all those years ago:

> Forbear, forbear or feel my power
> The Golden Cradle ne'er be got
> 'Til a mortal undaunted at midnight's mirk hour
> Nine times alone shall circle this spot
> When nine green lines shall encircle me round
> Then shall the Golden Cradle be found.'

By the time she finished, the sheer force of her words had brought Kenneth to his knees and all round him his men, all experienced warriors, lay flat to the ground, covering their ears with their hands. This made no difference and each one felt as if a great bell was ringing in his head as the chant continued. At last the chanting stopped and the king looked over the lochan. The gigantic female had disappeared but the wind still howled and the rain was coming ever harder. Gathering his men, the king headed back down to the fort of Druskin. He saw little point in trying to fight against supernatural powers – he had been victorious, the whole country was now his. What did he really need the Cradle for anyway, he thought to himself as he retreated down the hill.

None of those who were there that day could ever be induced to go up the hill above Abernethy again, including the King of Scots. Kenneth was a man who prided himself on his common sense, for all that he was a king, and he had no intention of ever again trying to face that monstrous being.

The story, however, flew around the country like wildfire and many people repeated the charm of the great carlin over the coming months and years. After a few years, first one then another would go secretly to the lochan and would walk nine times round the lochan laying a trail of green thread but always, always their work would be disturbed by wild storms and the return of the magical defenders of the place. Sometimes in the midst of the howling wind and blowing rain it was the great carlin herself, other times a dwarfish man with brown skin and long red hair and beard would come from the lochan in a conical cap and disturb the seeker. And though each one was all alone, just as was required according to the ancient chant, one reckless blade after another was thwarted in his quest for the ancient treasure.

One time a local lad, Matthew Muckly, who had gone off to be a sailor, came home to Abernethy. He was staying with his widowed mother and was having a grand time going out drinking with his old pals whom he hadn't seen for many years. Matthew had been very successful and, as they say, he wasn't short of a bob or two, which made him very popular in some quarters! One night near Hogmanay he was in a local tavern with his friends when the talk came round to the Golden Cradle. Now Matthew had forgotten all about the ancient story while he was travelling the seas but as soon as he was reminded of it, he decided he would be the one who would find the hidden treasure.

Fired up with a fair amount of whisky, he declared to the assembled company that he, Matthew Muckly, would head up the hill the following morning and would do everything that was required in the ancient spell. He would come back with the Golden Cradle of Abernethy for everyone to see. Given the fact that the whisky flowed even faster after this declaration it was a pretty soused Matthew that headed up to the lochan the next morning. With him went his old pal Tam Miller. They were both so full of drink that they paid no attention to the requirement that the seeker after the cradle should go alone. They figured that with the two of them their chances would be twice as good. By nightfall there was no sign of them and a party went looking round the lochan with torches but nothing was found then, or ever after, of Matthew Muckly and his pal!

Despite this tragic event there were still others who thought they could gain the treasure and all of them came to grief, one way or another. Jock Pitversie, a local carter, tried and was found wandering the hills a few days later, quite out of his wits. And he stayed that way the rest of his life. Another local lad, Tam Pitcurran, also had a go, and whatever happened to him in the night on the hill was never clear for he came back deaf and dumb! And to this day no one has found the Golden Cradle of Abernethy.

stories of the saints

st merchard

SAINT TO whom people prayed for many years in the Highlands was St. Merchard. He is believed to have been one of the first Christian missionaries to have come into the west-central Highlands, though whether as a follower of Columba or of the even earlier saint Ninian, who was said to have spread the Gospel among the Picts, we can't be absolutely sure. He founded several churches in the Glenmoriston area in the west of the Great Glen.

His main foundation was in Glenmoriston below the ancient hillfort of Dun Dreggan, where ancient stories told that the mighty Fionn MacCool slew a dragon. On his death Merchard left instructions that his body was to be placed in an ox-cart and the oxen set moving. Wherever they stopped, that was where he was to be buried. This is the same idea that St Kentigern used to locate his church, and it may be that here we have a reference to some forgotten Christian rite, though it might be an echo of something older.

Like several other saints, Merchard left a bell with miraculous powers behind him. This was kept in the church at Clachan Merchard and had the power to ring of its own accord whenever a funeral approached the kirkyard. One dark night the locals were awakened in the middle of the night by

Merchard's Bell. Several of them headed at once to the kirkyard, there to find the body of a freshly-murdered man. The murderer was found nearby and subjected to the justice of the time – hanging. Clearly the bell had significant power.

Again, like other early Celtic Christian bells, it was believed to have the power to fly back to its home if removed. Whenever it was installed in a new church it would fly back to Clachan Merchard. At last in the 17th century the old church collapsed beyond repair and a new one had to be built some distance away. The bell was left on a tombstone in the original kirkyard where it remained for over a century till someone, no doubt a stranger with no concern for tradition or local belief, came and stole it. It has not returned since then.

However, Merchard himself lingered in the area a long time. One of the clan laws that in some areas survived very late was the *each-ursainn*, the horse fine. The clan chief could levy this on a family which had lost one of its male members and it was derived from the old clan obligation to fight on behalf of the clan when called on to do so by the chief. But the old laws became abused over time and on one occasion the fine – livestock to the value of a horse – was being levied by the chief in Glenmoriston, MacPhatrick, on a distraught widow, long after the warrior function of the clansmen had ceased. The chief sent his law-officer to do the dirty

work and he took almost all the sheep that the
poor widow was left with, leaving her effectively
destitute. This was not the intention of any clan
practice, which tended to centre around what was
best for the clan, not the chief. The woman prayed
that night to St Merchard.

The same night as he lay asleep the law-officer
was awakened by a thunderous voice that declared
to him, 'I am great Merchard of the miracles,
passing homeward in the night. Declare thou unto
MacPhatrick, the widow's sheep will never bring
him good.' The terrified law-officer fell out of bed
and went to rouse his master and tell him what
had happened. The upshot was that the widow got
her sheep back and MacPhatrick never again tried
to turn old clan law to his own advantage. Would
that other lairds had been likewise restrained.

st cadoc and the pictish giant

NOW IT IS well known that at least some of the Picts
spoke a tongue akin to that of the ancient Welsh.
The same, or similar, language was spoken by the
tribes of the Britons in what was called Strathclyde
– the lands that ran from Dumbarton on the north
of the Clyde down as far as Carlisle – and also by
the people of the Gododdin, whose area stretched
far south from the lands that adjoin the southern
banks of the Forth. So it is no surprise that the

Welsh have held on to stories about the times when so many peoples throughout the island of Britain were united by their language. One of these stories is about the early saint, Cadoc.

Cadoc originally came from Wales but even in that far-off country he had heard tell of the magnificent Christian centre that flourished at St Andrews in the Pictish province of Fife. So he set himself to travel through Britain and spend time at the monastery there. After seven years amongst the Picts he decided to head home and traveled west through Fife, through the Gap of Stirling and into the lands surrounding the River Clyde. There he was asleep one night when a vision came to him telling him to go no further but to found a church on that spot and to spread the word of the Lord amongst the surrounding tribes for a further seven years. Being a devout and holy man he set to work at sunrise the following day, and after a few sips of water and a small piece of bread he began to dig the foundations of a new church.

He had hardly begun digging when he struck a great bone completely buried in the earth. Carefully he dug out the bone, a task that took him many hours. At last he had exposed the whole thing and found it to be a human collarbone, but so large that a man on horseback could have ridden through it. He was greatly amazed at this and realised that this must be the remains of a giant from the olden times. There and then he made a vow that no food or drink would pass his lips until the good Lord let him know just who this gigantic being had been. At that point, worn out by his digging, and the fact that he hadn't eaten that day at all, he fell into a deep sleep.

All at once another vision came upon him and he learned that the creature that had left this great collarbone would rise again from the earth at sunrise the next day. To Cadoc it seemed as if he woke immediately and as he did so the brightness of the dawn began to fill the sky. He sat up and looked around and there, no more than a few yards from him, sat a real giant, taller than the tallest tree he had ever seen.

'And who are you?' he asked the monstrous being, putting his faith in the Lord and being unafraid.

'I am Cau of Pictland,' replied the giant voice that rumbled like thunder and seemed to shake the very earth they sat on.

'And how came you here then, Cau of Pictland?' asked the monk, ignoring the rumbling in his own stomach.

'It was many years ago I came here over Mount Bannock,' rumbled the giant, pointing over his shoulder at the hills we now call the Campsie Fells. 'I was a wild and uncontrollable raider in those times and I had come to lift what I could from the lands around this river. But I met my match here and the local chief, who was near as big as me, slew me in battle and my bones have lain slumbering in the earth for hundreds of years, while I have suffered the fiery torments of Hell for my sins. And now the Lord has seen fit to allow me to return and to make reparations for all the sorrow I have caused on this good earth and has told me to do your bidding.'

As the great creature said this he smiled a smile of such sadness that Cadoc saw that truly his heart was pure and that he regretted his former wild life.

'Well then Cau of Pictland,' he replied with a smile, 'I think I know how to put your strength and size to good use. You can help me build churches to spread the word of the Lord among the savage tribes of this country.'

And so Cau of Pictland became the digger of the foundations of the churches built by the holy Cadoc and to this day we remember some of them in the names of places like Kilmadock near Callander and St Madoes on the banks of the Tay near Perth.

columba the healer

THERE WERE MANY tales told throughout Scotland of Colum-Cille of Iona, who nowadays we know as St Columba. (Though we know from history that he was a warrior and a politician as well as a priest).

Most of the stories concentrate on his holiness, though even in these tales he is clearly a man of considerable power. One of the poems attributed to him talks of his greatest fear being the sound of an axe in the Oak Groves of Derry. This strongly hints that he was well versed in Druidism or the ancient religion and he clearly had magical powers according to the stories the people told of him.

Not long after Columba had come to Scotland he was on the mainland preaching to the native Pictish peoples. His message met with some success and in many cases whole families were baptised together into the Christian church. One day a man came to see him, clearly distraught. Columba recognised him as one of those that he had converted with his whole family just days earlier.

'How can I help you?' asked the priest.

'O great master, it is my son. He has been taken ill and we fear that he is not long for this life if nothing can be done. Can you please come and help him?' replied the man.

When they came to his house, which was only a couple of miles away, Columba saw that there were several of the priests of the Old Religion there. They had come to berate the man and to tell him that his son's illness was the result of his converting to the New Religion – they had told him that the Old Gods had struck the boy down because of his treachery. As the priest reached the man's house the Druids were still there.

'You are too late, Christian,' cried one of them, 'the boy has died. Your power is of no use to you here.'

The man rushed in to the house and Columba heard his wife wail as she saw him. He followed in to the house to see the grieving parents sobbing in each other's arms.

'Though this seems hard to you,' the priest spoke, 'have no doubt of the power of the one true God who even now is watching over you. Where is your son's body?'

The mother raised her tear-stained face and pointed to a doorway, sobbing all the while. The priest ducked through the low doorway and there before him on a simple bed lay the young boy, about nine years old. At once Columba fell to his knees and began to pray fervently. The crowd of people who had followed him remained outside and they all listened intently as the sonorous Latin words arose from within the simple dwelling. On and on he prayed while the Druids stood outside and smiled at the assembled crowd.

All at once the praying stopped. In the small room where the boy lay, Columba rose briskly to his feet and in a stentorian voice that all there clearly heard, he commanded, 'In the name of the Lord Jesus Christ, arise, and stand upon thy feet.' By now the bereaved parents had come to the door and were peering into the room. As soon as the

priest had finished speaking they saw a wondrous
sight. Their poor, dead son opened his eyes and sat
up, looking around him with an expression of
puzzlement. He looked at his parents, then at the
priest, who held out his hand to help the boy up
from the bed. The boy took the priest's hand, rose
from the bed and was led out through the front door
of the house to stand before the gathered crowd. As
soon as they saw him the people there let out a great
cheer. Loud were the praises of the powers of
Columba and his god, as the Druids skulked off to
their retreat in the nearby forest.

st columba and the king of the picts

NOW WHEN COLUMBA had been exiled from Ireland
and came to Scotland he had been granted the use
of the island of Iona by the Pictish king, Brude, who
at the time was living in his great fortress in the
north at Inverness. After a time Columba thought
it a sensible thing to go and visit the king. Even if
he could not convert him he could at least ensure
that the Christian community could continue to live
on the island and preach amongst the Picts on the
mainland. When word came that the priest of the
new religion was coming the King's Druid Broichan
was intrigued. He had heard that Columba was a
man of power, but he was Druid to the king

himself and had little doubt that his powers would be a match for those of the Irishman. Columba knew well that he would have to deal with the druid at some point.

Not long after they had set out, Columba and his companions became aware that they were being trailed by a group of armed Picts. Whether they were sent out by a Pictish chief or some of the druidic comrades of Broichan, we cannot now be sure. There was little doubt, however, in the Christians' minds, when they saw themselves being followed by a substantial group of heavily armed men, that the strangers were up to no good. They were in no doubt that these men had been sent to kill them before they could reach the king's court and perhaps extract some privileges or promises from Brude. Now some say that Columba and his monks were not the sort to be afraid of a fight and that they went about armed. Whether or not that was the case, the saint knew what he had to do.

'Fear not, my brothers. The Lord will protect us just as long as you do as I tell you,' he said with a smile to the frightened monks. 'Gather round me in a circle and when I give the word I want you all to start singing the new prayer we learned last week.'

The monks looked at each other in astonishment. Surely he could not be serious! If they started to chant a prayer the warriors would hear them and fall upon them like ravaging wolves.

'Fear not,' said Columba, still smiling, 'come now and join me in the chant and all will be well.'

So there in the wild country of the Great Glen the small group of monks followed their leader as he started to chant. Less than half a mile away the Picts heard a noise.

'What is that?' asked their leader as they stopped to listen.

'Ach, it is nothing but the belling of some stags off in the woods,' said one of his companions, 'let's press on and catch up on the Christians. They must be a fair bit ahead of us if the stags are undisturbed.'

And so the armed warriors hurried on, passing close to where the monks were chanting, and soon they were far off. From that time on the monks themselves always called the new prayer Columba had composed for them *The Song of the Deer*.

It so happened that when Columba first came to the great fortress of King Brude at Inverness, the Pictish king was in no hurry to let him in. Brude wanted to see what this supposed great new priest would do. The priest and his companions had approached the great wooden double doors of the stone-built fortress and called out to be let in. When there was no answer one of Columba's companions ran and hammered on the great tree trunks that made up the massive door. Still nothing happened.

'Stand back,' ordered Columba.

As the monk stood back Columba went up to

the door, made the sign of the cross on the wood then laid his hands on the door. At once the bolts on the other side withdrew of their own accord and the massive doors swung back to allow the Christians entry.

Up in the great hall, a hundred paces back from the door, the king and his advisers heard the sound of the bolts withdrawing and a servant looking out of the hall door told them that the priest had entered the fortress. Taken aback at the obvious magical prowess of the stranger the king decided to take no chances and before the Christians were halfway to the hall, its doors swung open and the king himself came forward to greet Columba with all due respect, something that did not give pleasure to Broichan the Druid.

the irish slave girl

WHEN COLUMBA ARRIVED and made his representations to the king he noticed that Broichan had a young woman with him, obviously a slave brought on a raid from Ireland, whom he treated very roughly. Now it maybe was that Columba knew her or it may be simply that his heart was touched at her plight but either way, he resolved to do something about it. At the first opportunity he had, he asked Broichan to let the girl go free. The only reply was a contemptuous laugh. Now Columba was a man who was known to have a bit of a temper and, despite the presence of Brude and a retinue of armed warriors, he snapped back at the venerable Druid.

'Know this Broichan, if you do not let this girl go free here and now, you shall die before I have left the mainland to return to Iona!' he thundered. At this the colour left the Druid's cheeks, but he did not flinch and merely turned away with what he hoped was a contemptuous gesture.

Soon after this Columba and his companions left the fortress at Inverness and headed back down the River Ness towards Iona. They hadn't gone far when Columba knelt by the side of the river and picked up a small round, white pebble from the edge of the water. He held it up for them all to see and said, 'Behold this white pebble by which God will effect the cure of many diseases among this heathen nation. Now my friends, at this very moment Broichan is in extreme discomfort for an invisible angel has descended from heaven and, striking the beaker from his hand and shattering it, has left him barely able to catch a breath. We shall stop and rest here for the king has sent two messengers after us to ask if I will return and try to help the Druid, who now knows the power of the Lord.'

He was still speaking when the sound of approaching horses was heard, and within moments two messengers from the king came up to the group gathered by the Ness. The story that they told matched everything that the priest had said and the messengers finished by asking if the Great Columba would return to the court to help the ailing Druid. They emphasised that the king was very fond of Broichan and that it would be well to do as they asked.

Columba, however, had other plans. He simply sent two of his companions back to the court with clear instructions. If Broichan agreed to set the slave-girl free they were immediately to put the pebble in a beaker of water and give it to the old druid to drink. When Columba's companions got back to the fort and told the king what Columba had said, he was so impressed by the strength of character that had allowed him to send his companions in his place that he had the girl freed at once. The two monks then produced the pebble and put it in a beaker of water. At once the pebble floated to the top, causing gasps from the men of Brude's company who were with him. All there realised that there was great power in what was happening and the water was immediately given to Broichan to drink. He took one sip, then another, and began to sit up. He sat straight up and drank off the whole beaker of water and it was clear to all there by the colour in his cheeks that he was back to normal. Broichan was restored to health.

The stone had worked and was used as a cure

for many years, but it could do nothing for those whose allotted time had come. If sought at such a time it simply disappeared, something that happened when the king himself eventually began to approach his time in the fullness of his years.

a Battle of magic

IT IS THE way of things that sometimes when you do someone a favour you upset them. They feel as if they are in your debt and resent it. This seems to have been what happened between Broichan and Columba. There was no doubt that Columba saved the druid's life, but Broichan reasoned that he would not have fallen ill in the first place if it hadn't been for the meddling Christian priest. He resented the reputation that Columba had gained amongst the people after the incident with the pebble and was itching for a chance to even the score. When next Columba came to Inverness, Broichan asked the Christian when he was intending to leave. He had noticed that the Christians this time had come by boat and he had a plan to disrupt their departure.

'Well,' said Columba, 'I will be setting sail in three days from now, if God permits it.'

'Ach I don't think it will be down to your God,' smiled Broichan, 'for I will use my powers to raise unfavourable winds and a great darkness, and you will be unable to set sail at all.'

'All things are in the control of the Lord,'
replied Columba, 'what will be, will be.'

So after three days Columba and his companions
were ready to head down the river and on through
Loch Ness on their journey home. Out on a nearby
hilltop Broichan had been busy incanting spells and
not long after daybreak, when the Christian always
arose, the weather began to change. A great howling
wind came rushing up through Glen More and
heavy black clouds swept in, turning the morning
almost as dark as night. The waters of the river
surged as if in spate and it was clear that condi-
tions out on the loch itself must be dreadful.
However none of this seemed to bother Columba at
all. He prayed to Christ the Lord and got into the
small boat that was drawn up on the shore, asked
his companions to get in and told the sailor to
launch it out onto the loch. This they did but once
they were bobbing about on the seething waters
they were reluctant to raise the sails. Columba gave
them a straight order; 'Raise the sails, we are in no
danger here.'

As soon as they did what was asked a remarkable
thing happened. The crowd of people who had
come to watch what happened to this Christian
priest were astounded to see his boat sail straight
into the surging wind! Before they had gone a mile
in this miraculous fashion the wind dropped and
surged again, this time from directly behind the

boat, and the bystanders saw Columba sail out of sight down the Loch. Broichan's magic was powerful but it seemed that of Columba was even greater!

COLUMBA AND NESSIE

ANOTHER TIME COLUMBA had occasion to go north to Inverness. He and his companions were looking to find a way across Loch Ness when they came across a group of people near the shores of the loch who were burying the body of a young man. As they watched the proceedings one of Columba's companions, who spoke the Pictish language, asked a bystander what had happened to cause the young lad's death. He then informed the saint that the unfortunate lad had been swimming in the loch when a great snake-like creature had swum up through the waters and taken a great bite out of his side. The lad had managed to swim to the shore but died as soon as he got there.

Now Columba was looking over the loch and, spotting a small boat on the far side, he said to the monk who had translated for him, 'Look over there. There is a boat that can carry us over the waters of this loch. Swim over and row it back to us.'

The monk looked long and hard at the saint but, as he knew that Columba had power over the weather and almost every creature on the planet, he took off his robe and waded out into the cold waters of the loch. He had just started swimming towards the boat when a hundred yards before him the head of a great monstrous eel-like creature broke the surface of the water and made towards him. The funeral party saw what was happening and many of them let out great cries of fear and lamentation. Even some of Columba's companions fell to their knees and began to implore the Lord to save them from this monster. But even as the great scaly creature bore down on his companion the saint looked on calmly. Then slowly he formed the shape of the cross in the air with his right hand and called out in his sweet and powerful voice, 'Think not to go further, nor touch the man. Quick! Go back!'

The creature, which had reared up to strike at the swimming monk, stopped still in the water as if a spear had pierced it. The upper half of its long body was straight out of the water and its monstrous ugly head turned to look at the saint. It seemed forever that the great monster hung in the air, then it shook its head, turned and dived back under the water. The monk, at a sign from Columba, continued swimming to the other side and fetched the boat back. Then the saint and his companions crossed the loch and carried peacefully on their way, and nothing more was seen of the beast. Well not until over a thousand years later, though nowadays we call her Nessie.

the story of triduana

NOW TRIDUANA WAS a beautiful young woman
who, despite being sought after by many young
and not so young men, had decided to devote her
entire life to God. There are those who say that she
came originally from over the seas and she was
famous for her piety and devotion to God before
she settled as the Abbess at the ancient Christian site
of Restenneth, close to the ancient town of Forfar
in the Pictish province of Circinn. Such was her
renown that she soon came to the notice of the
Pictish king Nechtan, a man of strong passions.
Intrigued at the stories he was hearing of this
beautiful and pious maiden, he decided he should
go and see her for himself. So one day he and a
group of his men came to the Abbey at Restenneth
and asked to see the abbess.

Now, Triduana may not have been a worldly
person but when the king asks to see you it is always
a sensible thing to go along with the request and so
she came forth from the Abbey. It was a beautiful
sunny summer's day as she stepped out of the doors
of the Abbey to greet the king. He and his men
were standing a little way off as this beautiful
woman came out. Just one look, that's all it took,
just one look and Nechtan, the great warrior and
hero of a hundred battles, was smitten with love.

As Triduana came forward and made as if to

kneel before him he reached out and took her hand. She looked up into his eyes.

'No Triduana, do not kneel before me. I think you are the most beautiful creature I have ever seen and I would like you to be my queen,' he said with a smile. There were gasps of astonishment from his companions. Whatever was the king thinking of?

Triudana flushed, pulled her hands from the king's and, bowing her head, turned and scurried back into the Abbey.

Behind her she heard voices being raised. The king had thrown his advisers and companions into confusion. Triduana's face was flushed and her heart was pounding but she knew that although the most powerful man in the whole country had just asked for her hand, she had devoted her life to the Lord and there was no way that would change. Going in to a small chapel she used for her private devotions she knelt and prayed for a long time. At last she got up and asked one of the nuns if the king and his men were still at the front of the Abbey. The nun said they were and that the king was asking to speak with her.

'No. That cannot happen. You must go to him and tell him that I am a servant of the Lord and, though I appreciate what he has offered me, I am in thrall to something much higher than even he. Now go and tell him,' she said before turning and heading deeper into the Abbey building.

Now Nechtan was not pleased to get this

message, but he was not the sort of man to take no
for an answer.

'Ach, she's just unsure of what is happening,'
he told his companions, 'she is a nun after all. Let's
just give her a day or two and she will come round.'

So the king and his men set up camp close to the
Abbey and for the next few days he sent a messenger
to Triduana on the hour throughout the day and
night, asking to speak to her.

Now there are those who will tell you that
Nechtan was stubborn, but he was up against
Triduana who, once she had made her mind up on
anything, was utterly inflexible. She had dedicated
herself to Christ and no mortal man, no matter
how handsome or powerful, could ever change
that. So the situation continued for weeks. The
king would send his messengers and Triduana
would send them back with a refusal every time.

Throughout all of this Triduana was praying
for guidance from above but there was little help
forthcoming and she realised she would have to
resolve the situation herself. So one night after
having made her preparations she crept out of the
Abbey with just one nun and, mounting horses that
had been left ready for them, they headed west in
the deepest hours of the night. The nun was a local
woman and knew the country well and soon they
were a good distance from Restenneth. A day or so
later they arrived at Dunfallandy above the River

Tay, just a few miles south and over the river from the modern town of Pitlochry. Here there was a church that was attached to Restenneth and here she had decided she would hide out till the king gave up on his ridiculous idea of marrying her, a Bride of Christ.

For almost a week everything was peaceful, but there was no real hope of keeping anything secret from the king and at last a messenger arrived at Dunfallandy with word from Nechtan. He asked that she come back to Restenneth and if she would not he would come for her at Dunfallandy. There seemed to be no way out of the situation. She was standing there puzzling over what to do, when she saw another rider approaching at some speed. She looked closely and realised it was the king himself. Nechtan had become impatient to see her as soon as he had sent his messenger and had followed him on the road. He was clearly not going to take no for an answer. But Triduana was not going to agree to become his wife and as the king rode up and dismounted she ran off into the woods.

Nechtan came hard behind her and, realising she would never outrun him, the saintly nun climbed up into a blackthorn tree, tearing her robe and scratching her hands as she climbed. As Nechtan came up she sat on a branch of the tree and looked down at him.

'My king, this cannot be. I am a Bride of Christ

and have promised my life to the Lord,' she cried to him.

'But Triduana, I love you to the depths of my soul and I want you to be my wife and queen,' replied the king, dropping to one knee and holding out his hands towards her.

'O my king, what is it that you love so much about me?' she asked in a tone of some exasperation. 'Why do you pursue me so?'

'Ah, beautiful Triduana. The first time I saw your eyes I fell in love with you. You have the most beautiful eyes of any woman in the whole world,' the king replied with a smile.

'My eyes?' she asked, 'My eyes, that is what you love?'

'Well yes,' said the king, 'but . . .'

He had no chance to speak more for in an instant Triduana had broken off a length of branch and snapped it in two. Holding the two lengths of wood like skewers in her left hand she took her right hand and without a second's hesitation grabbed her right eye and plucked it clean out. As the king looked on in horror she stuck the eyeball onto one of the sticks and with no further hesitation repeated the process with the other eye!

'Here my lord king, here are the objects of the desire,' she said with a smile, holding the sticks down to him, even as the blood rushed from her sightless eye sockets.

Now Nechtan had fought in many battles and seen many gruesome things but this action almost made him throw up. At once he realised that this beautiful but devout woman would never succumb to his advances and, taking the sticks with their bloody eyeballs, he turned and walked silently away.

Triduana's companion came to help her down from the tree and tried to staunch her wounds, which in fact stopped bleeding very quickly. Returning to the church at Dunfallandy, Triduana was told that the king had headed back towards Forfar. She realised that it would be politic to move away from Circinn so as not to remind the king of his defeat and soon she and her companion were on their way to the Lothians. There they founded a church at Restalrig and there, through the power of God, Triduana's sight was miraculously restored. There she lived and after a long life of fasting and prayers at last she died.

It wasn't long after this that a young woman in the North of England, who had gone blind, was visited by St Triduana in a dream. In the dream Triduana told the woman to go to her well at Restalrig and, if she bathed her eyes in the water from the well, her sight would be restored. The woman, mightily impressed by this nocturnal visitation, made arrangements to be taken to Restalrig and, just as the saint had promised in her dream, her eyesight was restored! A few years later the same woman's young daughter fell and lost her sight as a result of banging her head. She too was taken to the well and her sight restored. After this the fame of the well spread over much of the island of Britain and right up to the Reformation in the late sixteenth century the well was a popular pilgrimage sight, particularly for those afflicted with eye troubles.

stories of the stones

the maiden stone

HE MAIDEN STONE sits almost in the shadow of Bennachie, once a holy site for the ancient pagan inhabitants of the area.

On its top is the breast shaped prominence that was called Mither Pap, an echo of the ancient goddess who was thought to inhabit the landscape itself. Nowadays with the fading away of the old religion it is called Mither Tap. The Maiden stone, a now sadly fading granite monolith, has left us a tale of another female, no goddess but a beauty who was sought after by many men in her time. This was the Maiden of Drumdurno, reckoned to have been the bonniest lass in at least five parishes. Suitor after suitor had tried for her hand but at last she had found a lad who she fancied and her marriage date had been set.

The day before the wedding the farmhouse of Drumdurno was bustling with activity. Herself, her mother, aunts and the close friends she had chosen to be her bridesmaids were all busy preparing food for the great event the following day. Her father was a man of some substance and standing in the area and he had laid on plenty of food and drink for what promised to be the wedding of the year! While the men were off seeing to the setting out of the great barn for the party to come the women concentrated on getting the food ready. Bannocks

and scones and cakes all had to be baked and the
kitchen was hot and steamy as batch after batch of
baking was done in the great farm oven. By late in
the afternoon all of the women were in need of a
rest and they retired through to the front room of
the farmhouse, a large and comfortable building
reflecting Drumdurno's years of prosperity. They
had made a vast amount of food, and the girnel,
the great chest where the oatmeal was stored, was
now only about an eighth full.

Not all of the women went to relax and rest
their feet, for the Maiden herself was too excited to
sit. Her head was full of thoughts of the morrow
and her handsome Davie, a young man with a big
enough farm of his own and the prospect of being
a wealthy farmer himself in time to come. But it
wasn't the thought of his wealth that pre-occupied
the Maiden as she carried on baking scones. She
thought of how she felt when he took her in his
strong arms and kissed her. As she thought of what
would happen once they had been bundled by the
guests and were left in their wedding bed alone, her
whole skin glowed as she blushed. She was a healthy
young lass and was full of the joys of youth. She
could hardly wait.

The heat of the kitchen was such that the
windows were all wide open and as she stood there,
kneading flour with her glowing skin and flashing
eyes, she was a picture of beauty that would turn

the head of any man. She was so rapt in her thoughts
of what was to come that she didn't notice that a
man had approached the window. All at once she
became aware that she was being watched. She
looked up and there at the open window was a tall,
dark and good-looking stranger. She gave a little
cry, as he stood there looking directly and boldly at
her, with a little smile playing around his mouth.

'Aye ye are workin awa brawly there, lass, ye
seem tae ken how tae bake richt enough, but maybe
you are no as fast as ye could be' he said in a deep,
dark voice that sounded like someone she had
heard before but could not place.

Realising she was standing with her hand at
her throat and her mouth open in surprise, she
thought she must look a right mess.

'And wha are ye tae creep up on a person like
that and whit dae ye mean A am slow at the bakin?
A'm as fine a baker as ye'll find anywhere,' she said
in a sharp voice, all the while noticing how good-
looking the stranger was. At that point she thought
of Davie and realised she must let this stranger
know what was going on.

'A'm bakin for ma ain weddin, tomorrow,' she
said, 'and A will hae it aw finished in plenty time.'

The stranger laughed and spoke again. 'Aye aye
maybe so, but A reckon ye'll have tae speed up a bit
if ye're tae be as good a wife as ye think ye will be.'

'How dare ye,' she said, 'Comin here an criticisin

me on the eve o ma ain waddin. A'll no hae any problem finishin whit a have tae dae, A'm as fast as A need tae be.'

'Aye right then,' the man said, smiling with his lips but his eyes darkening a little, 'A'll mak ye a bet. Ye see what ye have left in yer girnel ther?' he asked.

Unsure of what he was meaning she nodded, looking at him a bit askance. She had been flattered at his attentions for a minute but now she was a bit unsure of what was going on.

'Well A'll bet ye A can mak a raoad richt up tae the top o Bennachie afore ye can finish bakin aw the meal in yer girnel. Whit dae ye say?' he asked, and smiled, showing beautiful white teeth.

Giving herself a wee shake, the Maiden laughed. This was just some joke. Probably a pal of Davie's that he had sent to cause a bit of fun.

'Ach that's no a bet at all,' she replied, 'A'll easy win, but whit's the wager?'

'Weel if a can dae it, tomorrow, ye've tae be mine an no Davie's,' he said, still smiling, his eyes twinkling.

Certain now that this was a joke, she primly said, 'Fine, fine. A accept the bet. Now run along an let me get on wi ma bakin.' She looked down at the girnel and looked up. The stranger had gone without her noticing him leave.

She gave a wee laugh to herself and returned to her baking, and her thoughts of Davie and the

marriage bed that awaited her on the morrow.
She was lost in her thoughts for half an hour or so,
standing there kneading flour and doling out
bannocks. From through the house she could hear
laughter. Her mother and the rest of the women
sounded as if they had maybe had a taste of the
flagons of whisky that had been brought in for the
wedding. She smiled at herself and looked up
through the window. The daylight had shaded into
the long soft gloaming that makes Scotland's summer
evenings so magical and she thought she had never
seen the country look so beautiful. But what was
that? Up on the side of Bennachie was a dreadful
sight. There in the fading light she could clearly see
a brand new road, leading all the way to the Mither
Tap o' Bennachie. She gasped and at that moment
the stranger came into view. She now realised what
had happened. She had been tricked by the Devil
himself. She had agreed to the bet and had given
her word.

Screaming in panic, she ran from the farm
towards the Pitroddie woods. In the farmhouse the
women heard her cry but by the time they rushed
through to the kitchen she was gone. Into the dark
woods she ran, her mind paralysed by fear. She knew
that she should pray for help but no words would
come. Behind her she heard approaching footsteps,
getting louder till they seemed to echo through her
mind. Out of the woods she burst and just as she

reached the crown of the hill sloping towards
Pitroddie, her pursuer caught up with her. Laughing
viciously he reached out to grab the Maiden of
Drumdurno by the waist. Just as his hand closed
on her flesh he realised that instead of clutching the
warm, soft, firm flesh of the beautiful lass he had
lusted after, he was holding onto stone! He banged
into a great lump of granite, rooted to the ground
just where the lass had been a split-second before.
In his hand was a piece of that stone which had
broken off as he clasped his intended victim.
Somehow the prayer the Maiden had been unable
to even put into words had been answered. He had
been thwarted in his desires at the very last minute.

Although the lass had lost her life by being
turned into stone she had been spared the fires of
Hell and a great deal else besides!

martin and the dragon

ANOTHER PICTISH SYMBOL Stone whose carvings
might have inspired a local story is Martin's Stane
on the back road from Dundee to the village of
Tealing. Like some other such stones it has a serpent
and Z-rod carved on it as well as a mounted figure
and the Pictish beast, a truly enigmatic figure, a
little like a dolphin. The local tale has survived in a
short poem which tells of a great Dragon.

'It was tempit at Pittempton,

Draggelt at Badragon,
Stricken at Strikemartin,
An killt at Martin's Stane.'

One hot summer's day the farmer at Pittempton,
now on the northern edge of Dundee, was working
hard in his fields. He grew thirsty and called on his
eldest daughter, 'Daughter will you go down to the
well and draw me some fresh water. I am parched
working in this heat.'

'Certainly, father,' she replied and ran back to
the house for a pitcher. Moments later she came
out of the house and headed off to the well that was
out of sight from where the farmer was working.
Off she went and when after about a quarter of an
hour she had not returned, he thought he knew
what was going on. So he called on his next oldest
daughter and told her, 'Look, get up to the well
and tell your sister to bring the water I asked for.
No doubt she has managed to find that young lad
of hers, but tell her to get a move on.'

So she too went off to the well, thinking, like
her father, that her sister had run into Martin, the
young man she was hoping would marry her.
She was waiting for him to ask her father for her
hand in marriage. After a further ten minutes, and
by now getting a little angry, the farmer called on
the next daughter to go after her sisters and hurry
them up. She too went off, and again she did not
return. So one after another the farmer sent all his

nine daughters to the well. When even the youngest had not returned he was furious and had no doubt at all that they were playing a trick on him and he went to the well himself, where he expected to find them all together. Well they would get a piece of his mind for their stupidity, he thought to himself as he approached the well.

When he came to the well, he there saw a terrible sight. Round the well lay a great, coiled, dragon-like serpent. Scattered about were the bodies and limbs of his nine daughters. The beast had killed them all. He let out a great shriek and fell to his knees in grief and horror. Many of his neighbours were also out in their fields and they all heard the terrible cry. Immediately they all headed towards the sound, most of them carrying the hoes, spades and mattocks they had been working their ground with. In the front of the crowd was Martin, who somehow sensed that whatever was wrong involved the lass he loved. Alarmed by the great shriek he had picked up a large branch recently chopped from a tree and was carrying it over his shoulder like a club.

Seeing the crowd of people coming towards it the dragon shot off to the north, hotly pursued by Martin, who, when he saw the grisly remains of his lass and her sisters, felt as if his soul was seized with fury. The creature wriggled its way through the muddy hollow below Baldragon farm, still heading north. Martin ran like the very wind and

just as the great scaly creature got to the Dighty
Burn, he caught up with it and raised his club. The
following crowd yelled out as one, 'Strike Martin!'
and he gave the beast a crashing blow. This only
served to make it double its speed and it soon out-
stripped him. Help was at hand however, for horses
had been brought and soon Martin and several
others were in pursuit of the monster. Straight
north it headed with the determined group of riders
hunting it down. Soon they had it surrounded and
after a short struggle, killed and buried the fearsome beast. It is on this spot that tradition tells
Martin's Stane was raised and the village of
Strathmartine itself, close to Pittempton, is said to
have once been called Strikemartin! The old poem
commemorated what happened that day.

'It was tempit at Pittempton' – that tells of how
the dragon was tempted by the sweet young bodies
of the daughters of Pittempton's farmer. 'Draggelt
at Badragon' describes how it slithered through the
muddy hollow below Baldragon farm itself, and
'Stricken at Strikemartin' tells of Martin catching
up with the fearsome beast and clubbing it. The last
line lets us know of its eventual killing at Martin's
Stone in the shadow of Balluderon Hill to the
north of Pittempton. And even into the nineteenth
century people used to point out nine graves in the
kirkyard at Strathmartine as the last resting-place
of the nine sisters.

Other Pictish stones were once to be found in this area – one with a carving of a man with a large club over his shoulder; others, of which one is in nearby Dundee Museum, had serpents of different kinds on them. This suggests some sort of important Pictish centre here, perhaps a pagan temple or similar. What is certain, however, is that this is not the only story of the Nine Maidens. The hills to the north of the Stone have a different group – the Nine Maidens of Abernethy, who were known as Pictish saints. Other tales tell of similar events in Aberdeenshire, while there are Nine Maidens' Wells in many locations. There are also links to King Arthur and the Nine Maidens of Avalon, Apollo and the Nine Muses and the Norse god Heimdall who had nine mothers. Perhaps what we have here is a remnant of a memory of groups of ancient pagan priestesses. Whatever the Nine Maidens were, their hold on the public imagination lasted a long time.

the nine maidens of abernethy

BACK IN THE SIXTH century, at Piper's Den at the head of Glen Ogilvy in the Sidlaw Hills, there lived a man who has come down to us as Saint Donevaldus, probably originally just plain Donald. Now the Sidlaw Hills, originally known, as they still are locally, as the Seedlie Hills, run roughly parallel

to the River Tay from Perth to several miles beyond
Dundee. Their name is thought to be connected with
the Gaelic *Sith*, the People of Peace or the fairies,
and there are many strange stories told about places
in the Sidlaw Hills. But here at the top of Glen
Ogilvy, a bit apart from the rest of the local
community, Saint Donevaldus lived a simple,
contemplative life of hard work and prayer with
his nine daughters. They all worked hard in the
fields to grow their barley and it is said that they
lived on one meal a day of barley bread and water,
spending much of their time praying, fasting and
meditating. The old saint's reputation as a holy man
spread throughout his lifetime and when at last he
went to meet his maker, his daughters carried on
with the same simple life they had grown to love.
Soon they too developed a great reputation as holy
women. Perhaps they also had magical powers for
it is told that one day the eldest of the daughters,
Mayota, came out to their barley field to find that
a flock of geese passing overhead had been tempted
by the ripe grain. They were descending on the crop
just as she approached. It was a massive flock of
geese but Mayota simply called out in the name of
the Lord and told the birds to go elsewhere. At once
the entire flock of geese rose up as one and flew
away north, leaving the sisters' crop behind, never
to return.

As Mayota and her sisters carried on the life in

which they had been raised, their reputation as holy women just grew and grew. In the end, word of these devout lasses came to the ears of the Pictish King Gartnait in his capital at Abernethy. He was so impressed by what he heard that he sent his messengers to the holy sisters asking them to come and live at Abernethy. It was just about the most important Christian site of the Picts and he built them a small chapel on the north side of what is now the kirkyard of Abernethy. The sisters moved to the capital but continued to live a simple life of prayer and devotion till at last, after long lives, they passed away. It is said that they were all buried at the foot of a large oak there in Abernethy. In time they became very famous and wells were dedicated to them all over the east and north of Scotland.

Other versions of their story say that they initially came to Abernethy with St Brigid from Ireland but Brigid is simply the Christianised form of the much older goddess figure of Brid or Bride who is as much Scottish as Irish. Around Abernethy it was believed that she in fact did come to Abernethy in the far distant past, not from Ireland but from Glen Esk in the foothills of the Grampians. There are scattered Bride place names in the Glens of Angus to this day, but they are not St Bride's names. In his 16th century *History of Scotland* Jhone Leslie says that the Scots of his time believed that St Bride was buried in the Chancery of Abernethy.

OCHONOCHAR

IN ABERDEENSHIRE, many miles north of Martin's Stane, another version of the story is told. It was in the time of the Picts that a great warrior called Ochonochar, said to be the ancestor of the Forbes clan, lived on Donside, near Kildrummy. One year when the weather was extremely bad and people were near to starving, a great boar (though some say it was bear) came out of the forest and began attacking humans. Soon the whole area was living in terror of the fearsome beast as it killed their young women, one after another. Several men had been badly wounded by the beast but because all men went around armed in those far off times, and knew how to use their swords and spears, none of them had, as yet, been killed. Several men, singly and in groups, had tried to corner and kill the beast, but it had proved too strong, or too cunning, for them. Soon it had killed a total of nine young women in the area around Auchendoir. At this point Ochonochar came on the scene. He had been away from Donside for a while and came back to dreadful news. The great beast that was ravaging the countryside had killed his intended wife, Bess.

Now Ochonachar was a man who knew no fear and despite the warnings of his kinsmen that this was a fierce beast indeed, he immediately set off on its trail, stopping only to pick up an extra-long spear. Fired up with grief and anger he tracked the great beast to its lair near where the Woods of Logie now grow. There he came upon the beast lying at the opening of its den, gnawing on the bones of one of its unfortunate victims. He didn't hesitate but ran straight at the beast. Hearing him coming, the boar looked up to see this human charging at it. It rose on its feet and lunged at the man. Too late! As it thrust forward Ochonochar suddenly stopped and, bracing his spear's butt on the ground, tensed himself as the beast ran at him. The force of its powerful legs ran it straight onto the point of the warrior's spear. The spear ripped through its body and with a great squeal the vicious boar writhed its last breaths as Ochonochar held on to his weapon.

Now there are those who say that as the spear ripped the life from the great forest beast, Ochonochar cried out, 'For Bess,' and this is where the name Forbes comes from, but as to that you must make up your own mind. What is without doubt is that in the Woods of Logie there is the Nine Maidens' Well and at nearby Kildrummy there is the Nine Maidens' Green, where tradition says the Nine Maidens are buried. There are reports that there was also a Pictish Symbol Stone there, but this has not survived.

the princess stone

IN GLENFERNESSON, NEAR the River Findhorn, there is the stone known as the Princess Stone, which has a sad tale. Back in the eighth century the people of Moray were being subjected to increasing raids from the warriors called the Vikings. Coming over the seas in their magnificent longships from Scandinavia these Norsemen were warriors every bit as fierce and brave as the Picts themselves. Fergus, King of the Picts, was at Lochindorb Castle when he heard that there had been a great battle on the Moray coast and that the Vikings had triumphed and were heading inland. Immediately he sent word out into the surrounding countryside for every fit warrior to come to him, fully armed, at the castle. Soon he had a substantial force and set off to the coast through the Pass of Divie.

The Vikings, thinking they had disposed of the main Pictish force, were strung out along the coast and the Picts fell on them, driving them back towards the sea. The Vikings could not rally and were forced back to their ships drawn up on the sands. In order to make their escape a rearguard was formed and this was led by Harold, son of King Sweyn of Denmark. The rearguard managed to create enough time for their companions to get to their longships and sail off but those who were not killed in the battle were captured – this included Harold.

He was taken back as hostage to Lochindorb castle itself. Fergus, growing sick of all the slaughter that had been going on, had a plan. He sent word to King Sweyn that he was holding his son as a hostage and that he wished to discuss terms. Now diplomacy in those far off times took a bit of a while, with ships having to cross the North Sea to Denmark and back again, and all the while this was going on Harold was stuck in the dungeon at Lochindorb. Most Viking warriors would far rather fall in the heat of battle and be transported to Valhalla than be captured, but Harold soon found some compensation in remaining alive.

For you see, Fergus had a daughter, Malvina, who was in her late teens. She became curious as to what this foreign prince was like and decided to visit him. With the willing help of a couple of her handmaidens, who were her cousins, she managed to sneak down to the dungeon to have a peek at the Viking. Even by the flickering light of a torch she at once realised that this was a fine figure of a man. Tall, bearded, and with long golden hair he looked every inch the warrior, even as he sat in the gloom gazing up at his unannounced visitors. And he could not help but notice that the tallest of the three young lasses looking in at him was a fine figure of a girl with her long black hair and rounded figure. Both these young people had a few words of each other's language and they managed a fitful conversation. The upshot of it was that Malvina began to call down to the dungeon on her own over the next few days.

Things have a way of happening between young men and women that go far beyond the under-standable desires and wishes of healthy minds and bodies. In fact it wasn't long at all before the two of them looked forward to their all too brief meetings more than anything else. Now you can understand this on Harold's part – he certainly had time hanging on his hands, and he was always counting the minutes till he could see Malvina again, and always she was with him for far too short a time. When she wasn't with him she could think of little else other than the handsome Viking. As her mum was dead, it was just as well maybe that Fergus had matters of state weighing heavily on his head or he might have noticed that his beloved daughter was given to flushes and blushes and was extremely dis-tracted most of the time. If he hadn't been so busy hatching his own plans he might have noticed that his lass had fallen for the Viking.

As it was, she was terrified that he would find out. She did not know what was happening in the negotiations with the Danes, but she feared the worst. Many of her father's family had fallen in battle to the Vikings and she feared that her father had a terrible desire for vengeance against the Danes, for often enough she had heard him curse the day they

had ever come to Moray. Surely there was little
hope that Fergus would look kindly on her and
this foreign invader. As the weeks passed the pair
of them rapidly learned to speak each other's
tongues – love is always a great spur to such things –
and it wasn't all that long before they were declaring
their undying love to each other. Their physical
contact was restricted by the great iron gate of the
dungeon, though there were enough gaps through
which they could kiss and caress each other. This, of
course, only fired them up even more and it was
inevitable that Malvina would begin to lay plans to
set her lover free. She knew such an act would soon
be discovered but cared not for she was intent on
riding off with Harold as soon as she had him out.
She had gold and jewellery and was sure they could
get to a port on the coast where they would be able
to find some boat to take them, if not to Denmark,
then to Orkney where the Norse ruled. There they
would be safe until they could return to King
Sweyn's court in Denmark.

The plans were laid and with the help of her
cousins, Malvina organised a boat to take them to
the shore where a fast grey horse was waiting.
The problem of getting hold of the key to the
dungeon's great iron door was solved by one of
the cousins getting the guard on duty drunk.
The fateful night came. Carrying a small bundle of
clothes with her gold and jewels wrapped up inside

them, Malvina made her way to the boat. There in the faint moonlight was her Harold, free at last. The two fell into each other's arms in a passionate embrace, only to hear:

'Ssst, for heaven's sake, get off in the boat!' from the cousin who had let Harold out of the dungeon. Stopping briefly to embrace her cousin and thank her with a look, the young princess got in the boat with her Viking and at once he began to row them to the shore. It was a matter of minutes for them to cross the water, get up on the big grey stallion and disappear into the night. Somewhere on the hill of Aitnach they had a brief time together before heading down into the valley of the Findhorn and towards the sea. There had been more than a week of heavy rain and the river was in full spate. Morning found them approaching the village of Dulsie where Malvina knew there was a ford.

Behind them Lochindorb was in a tumult. The negotiations between Fergus and Sweyn had come to a happy conclusion. Fergus had proposed that Malvina and Harold be married thus cementing an alliance between the Men of Moray and the Danes, putting an end to the fighting for once and all. A messenger had arrived at Lochindorb before dawn with Sweyn's agreement and Fergus had gone at once to tell his daughter of his plans. She was nowhere to be seen and it was just as he stood at her chamber door that the alarm went up that the noble prisoner had escaped. Cursing at this unfortunate development Fergus gathered a group of warriors and headed off to the shore, finding the boat the couple had used abandoned there. So in the dark of night he and his men set off after the princess and her prince. It was clear they were heading for the coast and the pursuers made a good pace. In fact they made such speed that just as the sun rose fully they arrived on the hilltop above Dulsie. Down in the glen below they saw two people on a fine grey horse. It was them! A shout rang out, 'Malvina! Stay there. Stay there!' cried the king. Down in the glen the couple heard a voice but could not make out the words above the roaring of the river, writhing and twisting through the glen like a great snake-like beast. They turned to look at where the voice came from. There above them was a band of warriors and Malvina clearly recognised her father among them. Fearful of her father's anger and what would happen to her beloved man she cried, 'Now Harold, now! We must cross now before they come to capture us!'

It was well known that Harold, son of Sweyn, was a man of great courage and he did not hesitate but kicked his heels into the horse's sides and the great beast plunged into the seething water. Perhaps Harold was not the same master of a horse as he was of a ship, or maybe the water was just too wild, but immediately all three – Malvina,

Harold and the grey horse – were whipped away in the surging flow of the river. As her horrified father looked on from above the princess was torn loose from her lover and as he dived to catch her, the three of them – the two lovers and the horse – were all swept round a bend in the river and out of sight. All that day King Fergus and his men searched the banks of the Findhorn. Stopping only when it became too dark they resumed their search at daybreak and soon they found the bodies of the two young people, cold and dead on a shingle beach, but clasped in each others' arms. Priests were brought from the Picts and the Norse and a great burial ceremony was held by the banks of the Findhorn. The stone we still now as the Princess Stone was raised there in memory of the sad fate of two young lovers who never knew their union would have been blessed in two countries.

the king's three sons

THE MORMAER, or High Chief, of Ross was a hard and proud man. He was known to be a great warrior and a fine leader of men and such was his reputation that he had managed to secure the hand of the daughter of the King of Denmark. A great wedding had been held near the coast and the King of Denmark had sailed home with his three sons, thinking he had made a fine marriage for his daughter. Sure, she was living in Scotland, but he could always sail over himself, or send message for her to sail to Denmark, if he felt he needed to see her. This marriage with the Mormaer of Ross meant that his ships would have peace whenever they called in this part of Scotland and he felt that, in time, when grandchildren came along, things could only improve. The wars between the Danes – the *Fionn-Gall* – and the Picts that had happened so often in the past would gradually fade from memory.

However things did not turn out as he had hoped. Within just a couple of weeks the Mormaer showed his true colours to his new wife. He was in fact not hard but brutal and had taken to beating her whenever he was in a bad mood – which truth to tell was often. At first his wife put up with this harshness, hoping it would pass, but after a few months it was obvious that he was an overbearing and cold-hearted bully of a man and she wondered why she had ever even considered marrying him. In those days there was a great deal of traffic between Moray and Denmark and she managed to sneak a message out through one of her own serving maids to a Danish ship in the harbour. This was dangerous work, for if the Mormaer found out the maid's life would be forfeit, and likely that of the ship's skipper and his entire crew. Gladly, however, the maid returned to the queen safely and the following morning the ship sailed off for Denmark.

As soon as he had heard the story the Danish king set to organising a great fleet to come and avenge his own honour and that of his maligned daughter. Due to the recurring effects of an old battle wound he was in no fit state to lead the fleet himself, so he sent his three sons instead. They were seething with anger and could hardly wait to have their revenge on this foul wife-beater of a Pict.

So they set sail in their longships for Scotland in fine weather, hoping for a fast passage. The Viking longships were the finest sailing vessels of their day and in them the Vikings roamed as far as Africa and America. The seaworthiness of these beautiful vessels was matched by the skill of the men who sailed them, but seaworthiness and skill are of little help when the forces of nature unleash their fury. The three brothers and their fleet were still several miles off from sighting the Scottish coast when the weather turned. In the waters of the North Sea and the Atlantic the weather can change in minutes and before long they found themselves in a terrible storm. Despite their skill and the splendour of their ships the entire fleet was lost and the three brothers drowned. A day or two later after the storm had dropped, the bodies of the Vikings began to wash ashore along the coast of the Moray Firth between Nirth Sutor and Tarbat Ness. Among the bodies were the three brothers, whose fine clothing and personal possessions were recognised. The locals buried them with great honour and reverence and it is said that the wonderful Pictish Symbol Stones of Nigg, Shandwick and the Hilton of Cadboll were raised to show where they were individually buried.

SUENO'S STONE

IN FORRES ON the coast of the Moray Firth there is one of the most remarkable of the Pictish Symbol Stones. Standing almost five metres high it has been suggested that this stone is possibly later than all the other Pictish stones. It is a slightly different style from most of the rest but in its obvious depiction of a battle it is not unique, the other famous battle stone being the Aberlemno Kirkyard Stone, thought by many to be a depiction of the battle of Dunnichen, when the Picts slaughtered the Northumbrian Angles near Forfar in 685. In certain areas of Scotland the Pictish stones were long thought to be Danish and there is a strong connection with Scandinavia in the story of Sueno's Stone.

Though Sueno's Stone itself was found buried in the 18th century and then re-erected, the tale that local people told carries us back to what have long been called the Dark Ages. It is said that the stone commemorates a battle between the local people and an invading force of Norsemen. Fighting had been going on for many years as the Norsemen had started to settle in the area, and in the struggle for overall control of Moray the principal

antagonists were Maelbrigde, the Mormaer of
Moray, and the Norse Jarl, Sueno. Like Mormaer,
Jarl means something close to High Chief.

Now Maelbrigde was a famous warrior and was
known throughout Scotland, the Northern Isles
and much of Scandinavia as Maelbrigde Bucktooth.
This was because he had a strange deformity.
His left eye-tooth was almost ten centimetres long
and came down to just below his jawline. It was like
the fang of a wild boar and had a strange mottled
yellowish-reddish colour. It was rumoured that the
tooth itself was poisoned, and its size forced the
great warrior to speak with a bit of a lisp. It might
have even been this facial peculiarity that had
turned Maelbrigde into the fearsome warrior he
undoubtedly was. No one, Pict or otherwise, would
dare to pass comment on his tooth for his skill with
the sword was as legendary as his great strength.
Those who had mocked him in his youth did not
survive to tell their tale. He was a fierce and proud
warrior and his name meant 'The Servant of Bride',
the pagan goddess.

By this time Maelbrigde was into his middle
years and his face and body bore many scars from
battles with Vikings and Scots, and other Picts, for
they were a warlike people. He was more than a
great warrior, though. He was a true leader of men
and the Picts of Moray would follow him into the
gates of Hell if he commanded them. They had

grown to trust in this man's strength and wisdom and most of all in his skills as a strategist. In those far-off days a man's birth would do him little good if he could not wield a sword well and command the respect of his fellow tribesmen. And this respect was mutual. Bound as he was by blood-ties to many of the Picts in Moray, Maelbrigde felt it hard any time he lost a warrior in battle, and in the battles with the cursed Viking Sueno he had been losing fine young men, year after year.

All through one cold, wet winter as he sat by the fire in his fort by the sea, he puzzled over what he could do to resolve the ongoing feud. He well understood that Sueno was utterly ruthless and would be hard to convince that peace of any kind was a good idea. He was a Viking and thought the only options for him were victory or death. Still, he was a warrior and Maelbrigde thought he could settle matters once and for all. He would offer Sueno a straight fight, 'winner take all'. Whoever triumphed would have the overlordship of Moray. But Sueno would never agree to fight him one on one, such was Maelbrigde's fearsome reputation. Sueno was no coward but there were few men anywhere who would have reckoned they had much of a chance against the great Pictish warrior. At last he made a decision. He would offer Sueno a battle with twenty warriors apiece. That should make it all right. It was the warrior's way.

So the following day an experienced Pictish warrior called Drostan was sent to the Viking camp to carry Maelbrigde's challenge. Approaching the camp he held his hands high in the air to show he had no weapons.

The guards on the walls of the Viking fort, seeing he was unarmed, allowed the doors to be opened and two of them came out, battle-axes at the ready.

One of them spoke.

'What do you want, Pict?' he asked in Norse.

Drostan answered in the same language, for his command of it, learned from his mother, who was Norse, had made him the obvious choice for this mission.

'I want to speak to Sueno. I have a message from Maelbrigde.'

After checking to see that the Pict had no concealed weapons, the Vikings led him into the presence of their leader. Inside a large timber hall within the fort Sueno was sitting on a bench covered with furs. Drostan was led before him.

'Well?' demanded the Norse chief.

'My chief, the great Maelbrigde, has sent me with a message, Sueno the Viking,' the Pictish warrior said. He was a brave warrior who had faced death many times in battle, but standing here unarmed in the hall of the Viking chief he felt the cold drips of sweat roll down his back.

'Maelbrigde says that every year both you and

he are losing young men in these ongoing battles,'
he continued.

'So what?' snarled Sueno. 'What does Bucktooth
want to do? Does he want to surrender to me?' he
asked with a cold smile, well aware that using the
Mormaer's nickname would anger this Pict standing
before him.

Biting back a retort, Drostan simply bent his
head and said, 'Maelbrigde the Mormaer challenges
you to meet him in battle two weeks from the next
Saturday on the beach below the Red Cliffs at low
tide. He will bring twenty mounted warriors and you
will do the same. Whoever wins on the day will have
control over the whole of Moray. That is his
challenge. What is your answer?'

As the Pict spoke, Sueno's eyes had narrowed.
This was a straightforward challenge and was
certainly the warrior's way of doing things. However,
Sueno was never one to pass up any advantage so he
simply grunted, 'Tell Bucktooth I will think it over.'
Then turning to one of his warriors he spat out, 'Get
this piece of Pictish filth out of here.' Gritting his
teeth, Drostan was led out of the hall and through
the fort's gates. Later that afternoon he returned to
Maelbrigde's hillfort overlooking the Moray Forth.

'Well?' asked the Mormaer in his strange lisping
voice. 'What did Sueno have to say to my challenge?'

'I am afraid he said he would think about it,
that's all,' replied Drostan.

This was just about what Maelbrigde had expected. Sueno was a great warrior but it was well known that he always looked at every situation long and hard seeking to find an advantage.

'Well then,' Malebrigde smiled, 'we shall just have to wait.'

It was three days before an unarmed Viking turned up at Malebrigde's fort. On being shown into the Mormaer's presence he spoke, in Pictish: 'My lord, the great and famous Viking Sueno has deigned to accept the challenge you presented. Two weeks from this Saturday at low tide he shall meet you below the Red Cliffs. He shall bring twenty mounted warriors just as you shall. And he says he accepts that whoever wins on the day will have total control of all of Moray. Just as you suggested. And he swears this by Odin our All-father.' This last was said with something of a sneer but Malebrigde had what he wanted and he simply signalled for the Viking to be shown out.

In the week before the great battle the twenty chosen Pictish warriors were busy getting ready. Swords and spears had to be sharpened and polished, shields repaired and strengthened. As the day approached the excitement grew. The younger warriors were busy telling each other of how well they would fight on the day. The older ones just smiled and nodded. They had been in too many battles to take anything for granted. They were warriors, ready to die in battle as ever, and they knew their end could come at any time.

So the fateful day arrived and the twenty-one Picts rode out in a column from the hillfort to the cheers of the rest of the community. All were fully armed and all had carefully cleaned and combed their hair and facial hair. It was important a warrior looked his best on such a day. They made a magnificent sight as they rode down to the beach from the cliff-top fort, the cheers of their kin echoing in their ears.

As they approached the chosen spot below the great red cliffs, Maelbrigde could see a group of horsemen off in the distance. As they rode on he began to be able to pick out that there did seem to be about twenty of them. He scanned the cliffs above and the dunes below them. No sign of any extra Vikings there. He had been worried that Sueno might try some low trickery but everything seemed all right. On he rode and soon could clearly see that there were twenty-one horsemen approaching, the leader slightly ahead of the rest. But wait a minute. What was that?

On the back of every horse he could now clearly see two pairs of legs. The scheming conniving Viking had brought twice as many men as had been agreed. Maelbrigde's anger surged up through his blood. A red mist flared before his eyes at this treachery. Hauling out his sword, he waved it over his head,

kicked his heels into his horse and shouted charge.
Behind him the Pictish warriors reacted as one and
followed on after their leader. The Picts charged
straight into the Vikings. Just before Maelbrigde
and his men reached them the men behind the
riders leapt from the horses' backs and fanned out
to surround the Picts. Each and every one of them
was carrying a spear as well as his sword. As the
two groups of horsemen clashed the other Vikings
ran in at the exposed backs of the Picts.

It was over in minutes. Thanks to their leader's
treachery the Vikings had attained a remarkable
victory. All twenty-one Picts lay dead on the sand.
A few of the Vikings were injured but none had
life-threatening wounds. Even the great Maelbrigde
Bucktooth had been unable to kill any of them, such
were the overwhelming numbers and careful planning
of the Vikings. They were ecstatic. Their leader's
plan had worked and all of them had come through
the battle alive. Their comrades were treating the
few that had received serious wounds while the
others shouted and congratulated each other. Sueno
was looking down at the dead body of his opponent.
He had tricked the great Maelbrigde Bucktooth and
now he would be lord over the whole land of Moray.

With his sword in his right hand Sueno reached
down and grabbed the long hair of the Pictish
corpse. Yanking on the hair he pulled the upper
half of the body off the ground. With one stroke of

his sword he sliced of the Mormaer's head! His men saw what he was doing and let out a cheer.

Sueno held up the blood-dripping head of his enemy at the level of his own face and laughed at it, 'Well, what do you think of that trick then, Bucktooth?'

All around him his men burst into laughter, partly out of relief, partly to cover the embarrassment they all felt at the underhanded trick they had played on the Picts. Still the victory was theirs.

Then one of them, emulating their leader, reached down and lopped the head off another Pictish corpse. Whoops of laughter rang out again and another copied him. Within seconds all twenty-one Pictish corpses were headless. One or two of the younger lads among the Vikings started throwing the heads at one another and a couple of them began kicking them around. And all the while Sueno was looking at Maelbrigde's head with a smile on his face.

Then, sheathing his sword, he took the long hair of the Pict in two bunches, tied them in a knot and walked over to his horse. There he hung the severed head over the pommel of his saddle! His men looked at each other – he was going to take the Pict's head home as trophy of war. Some of them had heard the Picts themselves had once done such things. It seemed a good idea and the others started doing the same. Soon all forty-two of the Vikings were sitting on horseback, and half of them had blood-dripping, gory trophies of war hanging from the saddles of their horses.

And so off they set towards their own home base. Sueno, at the head of his men, could hear them begin to sing short snatches of songs and chant short lines about the great victory they had had. If he had a big head before it was even bigger now as he heard the singing and praises of his warriors riding behind him. So they set off along the beach towards home. But unnoticed by Sueno, caught up as he was in the success of his plan and the praise of his Vikings, each time his horse's hooves hit the sand the bloody severed head of the Pict turned just a fraction. It was a tiny movement each time but within a few minutes the long, discoloured buck-tooth of the Pictish leader was against the thigh of Sueno. He did not notice a thing.

Behind him several of his warriors had taken out the horns of mead they had brought and passed them round. The singing grew louder and Sueno's heart swelled. Truly he was great leader. This was just the start. Now he had gained control of Moray he could start to build up his power. Soon he would move on Caithness and after that, well, the opportunities were immense. Soon the troop of horsemen were in sight of their own palisaded fort. All along its ramparts the women and children and old men were lined up waiting to see how many of their husbands, fathers and brothers had survived the battle. When they realised that all forty-two of them had survived the whole community let out a great cheer. No one had been killed, they had all lived to tell the tale of a great victory.

On hearing the cheer Sueno hauled on his horse's reins. The great creature rose up on its rear legs, its forelegs pawing at the air. Then the Viking leader dug in his heels and the horse set off in a great leap. Through the air it soared and came down with a thud on the sand. And as it came down the force of its landing sent the head of Maelbrigde up in the air. Down it came. The tooth, the dis-coloured fang of Maelbrigde Bucktooth, sank its full length into the thigh of Sueno the Viking. He let out a dreadful shriek. He dropped the horse's reins and yanked the head up. Out came the ominous fang, followed by a great gut of blood. The watching crowd fell silent as Sueno threw the bloody head away from him with a roar of anger. Some of the warriors came to Sueno's help. The blood was pumping out of his thigh as he roared with the pain. 'This was not how a Viking warrior should behave,' some of them were think-ing. He was dragged from his horse, a tourniquet was improvised from a sword belt and a group of the Viking warriors carried their stricken leader back to the fort at a run.

Once there, they called the wisest and most

experienced of the old women to see what they could do. They came with poultices and bandages but as soon as the tourniquet was released the blood pumped again. And all the time Sueno roared like a madman. Mead was brought and he grasped the horn and tossed it down.

'More mead,' he shouted, as the women tried to staunch the bleeding. It took them a good while but at last they stopped the blood flowing, by which time Sueno had drunk so much mead he had fallen into a fitful seep. So they bandaged up his leg, and covered him with furs as he lay there tossing in a mead-induced stupor, muttering and moaning. This was bad. No Viking should act as he had done. It was only pain, and their warriors were raised to laugh at pain and death.

All through that night, with the old women watching over him, Sueno tossed and turned, pouring with sweat. Just before dawn he calmed down and seemed to have gone into a healthier sleep. Then in the morning they decided to look at his leg. As they pulled back the blankets and undid the bandages a dreadful, charnel house smell erupted. Tugging off the sodden cloths they all stood back. From the tip of his toe to the point of his groin Sueno's leg was black!

None of them, not even the eldest, had ever seen anything like this. It was as if his leg had been rotting for days! Maybe the rumours they had all heard about Maelbrigde's tooth being poisoned were true after all. Whatever the truth of the matter nothing could be done and by that night Sueno the Viking had breathed his last.

News of his death spread like wildfire amongst the peoples of Moray, both Viking and Pict. The news was passed onto men heading for Norway on board ships, and riders headed out with the tale to the west and south. And all carried the same story. Sueno the Viking had been deserted by the Gods of the Vikings. They had allowed Maelbrigde to have his revenge even after death because of what Sueno had done. By accepting the challenge to fight with twenty men and bringing twice that number, he had broken the word of the warrior and destroyed the code of honour that held a warrior's way of life together. By his treachery he had managed to kill the Pictish Mormaer and his men, but at a terrible price. From that day forth none of the men who had accompanied him on the fateful day below the Red Cliffs would admit to it and soon the Picts had re-established total control over Morayshire. And the local people said this is why the great stone was erected, to remind future generations of the treacherous behaviour of Sueno the Viking.

fight with an eagle

AT STRATHPEFFER THERE is a magnificent Pictish
Symbol Stone generally known as the Eagle Stone.
Some say that this the Eagle of Foulis, the crest of
Clan Munro, and there are even stories that the
stone was erected after a battle between the
Munroes and Donald of the Isles on his way to the
fateful Battle of Harlaw in 1411. Nowadays we
know the stone was carved much earlier than that
and there are stories that link the Eagle Stone to
the distant past.

In the olden times when people lived in small
clachans, raising cattle, growing simple crops and
hunting and gathering to support themselves, everybody was raised among their own kin. The kinship
groups of the Highlands gradually developed into
the institution of the clan, and in Strathpeffer the
man who became the first chief of the Munroes
had made his home. There in the shadow of the
great ridge of Knockfarrel, with its ancient fort,
there was a clachan, or wee village. Life was hard
for much of the time, though in seasons of plenty
the capacity of the people for having fun was as
great then as it is now. Their lives might have been
simple in some ways but they had music, poetry
and song celebrating their ancestors, the land they
loved and the history of their own kin.

For several years after Munro became chief, the

people kept an eye out for a great eagle that had its home at the top of an inaccessible pillar of rock on the side of Knockfarrel. Many thought it was a fitting sign, that an eagle – the king of the birds – should fly over them, for they were proud people and the men in particular liked the idea of this magnificent bird, symbol of strength and fearlessness living in the strath. The women were not so sure, and several of them had cursed the bird as it lifted a lamb or a goat kid from the flocks. Munro himself and the older warriors reckoned it a small price to pay to have such a powerful creature nearby. In those far off times when all were pagans, the magic power of beasts and birds was still recognised, and in general people lived mush closer to nature than we can even conceive of. In fact Munro had decided that the eagle would be his personal symbol and hoped that it would become a powerful symbol for all who were related to him.

However, his idea of the eagle was changed one late summer's day. It was at the time when the nights were just beginning to shorten and the days beginning to cool, although it was still sunny. A wee boy, about eighteen months old and just beginning to toddle about the place, was sitting playing not far from the door of his parents' house. His mother was no more than a few feet away talking to a neighbour as she did some sewing. Suddenly a great shadow fell over them and they looked just in time to see the great eagle swoop. With no sound other than the beating of its wings the great bird scooped up the wee boy in its vicious claws and in an instant was soaring back into the sky.

The boy's mother let out a terrible scream and fell in a dead faint. At once her neighbour began to shout for help. From all around the clachan people came running. Some had been working in the fields and were carrying their tools as if they were weapons, not knowing what had provoked the noise. One of the first to arrive was Hugh, the chieftain of the Munroes. He arrived to find several women beginning to lift another of their number from the ground.

'What has happened?' he demanded.

'It's the eagle,' replied one of the older women. 'It just came out of the sky and plucked wee Lachlan straight up. We were no more than a few feet away and we never heard a thing. Oh, poor Mina, to lose her bairn is such a way!'

All around there were mutterings of sympathy but Hugh was aware that several of the women were looking at him directly, waiting to see what he would say. More men and women came running up to be told in subdued voices of the great tragedy that had happened. Just then a young lad of no more than twelve years came running up.

'I saw it, I saw it!' he cried, his eyes almost bursting out of his head with excitement. 'I saw it,' he cried again.

'Calm down now, lad,' said Hugh. 'What did you see?'

'I saw the eagle,' the boy panted, 'It had wee Lachlan in its claws and it flew straight back to its eyrie. I saw it.'

Now everybody was looking at Hugh. He was the chieftain of the tribe – it was up to him to decide what to do. Luckily the one thing about the young man that everyone knew was that he could make up his mind in a flash. He knew exactly what he had to do.

He turned to one of the men close by, his brother-in-law, and said, 'Go get me a rope, as long as you can find.'

At once some of the men understood. He was going to try and climb up to the eagle's eyrie.

'Och Hugh, you're not to try and climb up to yon eyrie, it's impossible,' one of the older men put it to him.

'No, it's not impossible. Hard, maybe, but not impossible,' replied Munro, and all there could tell by the steely look in his eye that his mind was made up and there was no point whatsoever in trying to change it.

The rope was brought and, along with a group of other men, he headed off towards Knockfarrel. A bunch of the children attempted to follow but were brusquely sent back to their homes. The community had already lost one soul that day and there was a good chance they could lose another.

Soon they were at the foot of the great pillar of rock. Without a word Hugh stripped off his kilt, put the coiled rope over his shoulder and set off upwards without a glance back. All of his energy and thinking were concentrated on the matter in hand. What he was attempting was extremely dangerous and he knew if he let his mind lose focus for even a split second he could easily fall to his death.

So in total silence, broken only by the screeching of the great eagle far above, he began his climb. Up and up he went, using the rope now and again to lasso a handy projection of rock. Sometimes he had to go the left, sometimes to the right, but all the time he was getting higher and higher. He was more than half way up, his every move watched intently by his kinfolk on the ground below, when the great eagle flew off from its eyrie. A warning cry came from below and he hugged the rock as tightly as he could. Here on the rock face, clinging for dear life with both hands, he was an easy target for the great bird. Its vicious beak and sharp claws would be able to tear into him at will if it came at him now. But it soared up and away. Below, the others watched as it began a great circle hundreds of feet up above its eyrie.

Drawing a deep breath and gritting his teeth, Munro climbed on. Soon he was close enough to make out the individual branches and strong twigs that made the platform of the great bird's nest.

On he went, and he was about ten feet from the
eyrie when he heard a sound. It was Lachlan,
cooing away to himself as he crawled to the edge
of the eyrie. He wasn't only alive – he seemed
unhurt as well. Hugh peered up – it was amazing.
The great talons of the eagle, that could rip apart a
deer, could also carry this child in the tenderest of
embraces when necessary.

Hugh breathed a great sigh of relief. The laddie
was alive. Now, though, came the hardest bit.
Slowly and carefully he clambered up the last few
feet of the pinnacle. He did not look down,
knowing fine well that the sight of hundreds of feet
of nothing but air would do him no good. Slowly he
inched up; then he was at the edge of the platform.
Steadying his feet, he leapt upwards and sprawled
on the eyrie. His impetus made him bump into
Lachlan and the wee fellow rolled toward the edge
of the eyrie. Quick as a flash Hugh reached out
and grabbed the boy by his ankle. The wee lad
started to laugh! He thought this was all a game!
He didn't know the danger he was in, hundreds of
feet above the hard ground and exposed to the
elements on this platform in the sky.

But it wasn't the elements he had to worry
about. Again a cry came up from below and just as
it did Hugh heard the beating of enormous wings.
He looked up in time to see the eagle swoop towards
him, talons outstretched. Snatching a sturdy branch

from the eyrie he swept it at the great eagle just as it was about to strike. His blow caught it on the right leg and it spun away, screeching wildly. Again it came at him and again he swept at it with the branch, this time missing it, but it drew back once more. Again it came, again and again. Each time Hugh beat it off with the stick and all the time wee Lachlan was sitting at his feet laughing away – he thought this was great fun. But it was no fun; it was a life or death struggle. Down below the watching men realised what was beginning to go through Hugh's mind. If things went on as they were the bird would simply keep coming at him till he was too tired to fend it off! There was no choice. He had to take the initiative.

When the eagle swooped in again Munro dropped his branch. As the eagle stretched for him he reached up and grabbed its legs, above the razor-like claws, and pulled the creature down. Taking it by surprise, the man used all his strength to wrestle the great bird to the surface of the eyrie. The wee boy started to cry but Hugh paid him no mind. Throwing his body on top of the creature as its great wings battered at his head, he let go of its legs and took the creature by the neck. Its talons dug into his body and its wings thudded against him, but Hugh thought of nothing but the strength of his hands as he squeezed. He had no idea how long he lay there being lacerated and battered but

at last he felt the creature weaken slightly.
Summoning up the last of his strength he increased
his grip and felt the life drain out of the great eagle
he had pinned below him. At last it lay still and he
rolled off of the body taking great gulps of air,
hardly aware of the infant now clutching at his legs
as he lay there exhausted.

He reached out feebly and ruffled the wee lad's
hair and his crying began to quieten down. As the
laddie crawled up onto his chest and he cuddled
the distraught child to him, he began to realise
what he had done. He hadn't given the matter any
due consideration. He had made up his mind what
to do and had done it. He must have been mad! At
that he let out a laugh. Mad, maybe, but he and
the child were still, miraculously, alive. Faintly he
heard noises as if from far off. What was that?
Then he realised that the men on the ground had
no idea what had happened. All they had seen was
the flapping of the great wings and a great deal of
thrashing around, then – nothing. So, kissing wee
Lachlan gently on the top of his head, he put him
down gently in the centre of the eyrie. He got to
his knees and looked at the body of the great eagle
lying sprawled there. It was huge. The wingspan
alone must have been seven feet! At that the release
of tension, the relief of survival and the joy of
victory surged through every inch of his body.
Grabbing the great inert body in both his hands he

leapt to his feet holding the dead bird high above his head. Down below a great cheer rang out. With the strength coursing freshly through his veins he raised the bird even higher and threw it from the top of the great pinnacle. And as he released the body of the beast a great surge of wind caught it and it twisted and spun through the air till it landed back at the clachan, right where the Eagle Stone now stands. It was as if all the old goddesses and gods of the land had arisen once more in honour of the great deed of bravery that day. And that is why to this day there is an eagle carved on the stone at Strathpeffer.

In truth, climbing down the pinnacle with the wee lad tied firmly to his back was every bit as dangerous and magnificent a feat as getting up there, but he never spoke of it. And from that day on, if they hadn't known before, the people of the wee clachan in the shadow of Knockfarrel knew now that they had a true and worthy chief in Hugh Munro, a real hero.

stoneputter's challenge

NOW IN THE real old times Fionn MacCool and his warrior companions the Fianna used to live in the great fort on the summit of Knockfarrel. From here they would head out on their great hunting trips all across the north of Scotland. The Fianna were much, much bigger than the biggest humans today but they were not the only people of considerable stature in Scotland in those times. Not far off from Knockfarrel there lived a giant. Like many of his kind he spent a great deal of his time standing on his own hill and throwing giant boulders all over the country. This is why Scotland is covered in so many massive stones and from their number it would seem these giants were truly committed to their sport! Anyway, the giant was aware of the reputation of these supposedly great heroes living in Knockfarrel and decided he would challenge their leader to a contest. And what other kind of contest would a Scottish giant want to take part in but chucking boulders? He himself was so well known for this activity that they called him Stoneputter.

One day he turned up at the great gates of Knockfarrel and shouted out his challenge. Now Fionn was a man who had a considerable opinion of his own worth and he didn't see why he should have to stoop to taking part in a contest with a simple local giant. After all he was Fionn MacCool, famous in many lands for his courage and strength. So he asked which of his men would take up the giant's challenge. And having seen that Fionn himself would not deign to compete with such a creature, none of the warriors could see why they should be put in such an undignified position. While they were discussing this, Stoneputter was at the great gates of the fort bellowing out his challenge, and after a while beginning to hint that the inhabitants of the fort might not be all that they were reputed to be.

This was serious. Fionn couldn't put up with having his own honour and that of the Fianna called into question. Yet he had said he would not dignify the giant with a response and could not back down in front of his men. Nor could he command any of them to do a thing he would not do himself. That would truly be dishonourable and could lead to a lot of trouble! Now, Fionn had an odd knack. If he needed to understand anything he simply had to bite his thumb. He had, as a boy, burnt his thumb on the Salmon of Knowledge he was cooking for a Druid. The upshot of that was that he could access all the wisdom of the ages, and even see the future a bit, just by biting his thumb.

He was just about to do it when his dwarf spoke up.

'Och, Fionn, why not let me take on this giant? I can soon shut him up, no doubt,' growled the dwarf, in his deep, rumbly voice. At once Fionn saw the sense of this and sent the dwarf out to confront the giant. Now he might have been a dwarf amongst the Fianna but he was bigger than any man around is these days. Still, he hardly reached the giant's waist.

'A challenge is a challenge,' thought the giant,

certain he would beat this little one and demand a
better man the next time. He was sure he could
keep beating the Fianna till at last Fionn himself
would have to come out and have a go. Stoneputter
too was a creature with a high opinion of his
own worth.

'All right then,' he shouted at the dwarf, and
picked up a great boulder – one that three normal
men would not be able to move – and threw it high
into the air. Out and out it soared from the summit
of Knockfarrel, and came to the earth with a great
thud just at the eastern edge of where Strathpeffer
now sits. (This is the stone the Picts later carved
with the eagle).

'Huh,' grunted the dwarf, 'You think that's
something? Watch this.'

And with surprising speed he ran to the great
gates of Knockfarrel and one after the other he
pulled out the massive stone posts – neither of
which could be lifted by seven human men – and
threw them one after the other to land on either
side of the first stone. Stoneputter was crestfallen
and slunk off. He had come to defeat the great
Fionn MacCool and had instead been beaten by
the hero's dwarf. He would never live it down!

And for those who doubted such a story, it was
the custom of the locals to take them to the Eagle
Stone and there, on one of the stones alongside,
was the clear mark of a giant thumb and forefinger.

vanora's stone

ANOTHER PICTISH SYMBOL Stone with a remarkable story is in the wonderful little museum of Pictish Symbol Stones in the Strathmore village of Meigle, 20 kilometres north-west of Perth. Among this magnificent collection of Symbol Stones, which clearly point to an important religious centre nearby, is the great Cross-slab known to locals as Vanora's Stone. On the side opposite the magnificent Cross there is a scene which has been interpreted by various learned commentators as representing Daniel in the Lions' Den. It shows a gowned figure flanked by four-legged animals with heavy shoulders or manes. Many Pictish Symbol Stones clearly show both Christian and pagan symbols, and in basically pre-literate societies it is at least feasible that older stories could be attached to Christian symbolism. The Picts, like all early peoples, had their own mythology and beliefs.

Vanora's Stone is unusual in that it once formed part of a complex linked monument of different stones, though we sadly have no clear idea of how it used to look. The story told locally is that Vanora was the wife of the great king, Arthur. Having defeated his enemies and ruled peaceably for many years, Arthur decided to go on a pilgrimage to Rome, leaving his nephew Mordred as regent. Hardly had he set out when Vanora became involved with

Modred, and they began to rule the land together. Whether Modred seduced Vanora or it was the other way about is unclear, but they ruled as man and wife with the support of Modred's own Pictish troops.

Arthur was still in Britain when he heard the news and immediately headed north to raise his own followers and remove the usurpers. The battle where Mordred and Arthur met is said to have been at Camlann, on the Forth, somewhere around the year 540. In the fighting Mordred was defeated and killed and Arthur was fatally wounded himself. Though victorious, he soon passed away. Vanora was imprisoned in the great Iron Age fort on nearby Barry Hill while her fate was decided. She was not only guilty of adultery but had betrayed the king and thus the people – breaking a sacred trust – and her death was a foregone conclusion. Such was the blackness of her deeds, the story goes, that the wise men and priests who considered her fate decided she should be made to suffer as dishonourable a death as possible. So it was decided she should be torn to death by a pack of wild dogs and the sentence was duly carried out. This is how the locals interpreted the scene on the Cross-slab. Following her execution, her body was buried with oaths and imprecations being heaped upon her in a manner very suggestive of ancient pagan practice. This burial is said to be in Vanora's Mound in the kirkyard of Meigle and it was believed until recently that any young woman foolish enough to stand upon Vanora's Mound would be made barren, such was the power of the imprecations and curses heaped upon it so long ago. This was clearly not known to a local photographer who quite recently had the habit of posing newlyweds on the mound for photographs!

There are many places in Scotland that bear the name of Arthur – Arthur's Seat in Edinburgh, Ben Arthur in Cowal, another Arthur's Seat further up Strathmore from Meigle, and a handful of others scattered in the landscape around Meigle. This is hardly surprising, as the mythical Arthur was almost certainly common amongst the traditions of all the P-Celtic speaking tribal peoples of Britain. In modern terms these languages survive as Welsh and Cornish, as well as Breton. Accurate information can last for hundreds and even thousands of years through oral transmission and the idea of Arthur belonging as much to Pictish Scotland as Wales or Cornwall is not really strange at all, even though the Pictish language itself died out over a thousand years ago.

st orland's stone

NOT FAR FROM Glamis Castle stands a Pictish Symbol Stone long known as St Orland's Stone. Though it is unclear who exactly St Orland was, or even if he

existed at all, the local people thought that the stone
had considerable powers and that it could help to
foretell the future. It was a common occurrence for
girls in their teens to come to the hallowed ground
around the stone at the witching hour of midnight
to consult this ancient oracle as to who their future
partner might be. Whether the stone was supposed
to speak itself or whether the supplicant heard a
message in their own head is unclear but the tradition of consulting the stone went on generation
after generation. It was also where young lovers
would come to swear undying love to each other.

One time a local lass, the daughter of the butler
at Glamis Castle, a lass with a bit of 'a sense of
herself' as they say, had recently jilted the local
miller's son and had taken up with the minister's son.
Now, he might have been a son of the manse, but
he was still a young man and as capable of mischief
as all his kind, then and now. He was also a bit
unsure of his relationship with Jeannie, as the
young lass was considered both a beauty and a
good catch. The minister's son, Willie, was certain
it was only a matter of time before he too was
jilted by her. In fact, Jeannie really liked him and
thought she might even be in love but was a bit put
off by his sudden changes of mood. The more they
saw of each other the more she liked him but the
more he became worried that she was going to
leave him. This preyed on his mind so much that

he decided to play a trick on her, hoping to ensure she would eventually marry him. He kept suggesting that she should go and consult St Orland's Stone to find out what the future held.

Now, Jeannie was a sensible lass and thought all of the stories about the stone were a load of nonsense, and she was a bit taken aback that a minister's son would be urging her to get involved in such rank superstition! However he kept on at her and at last she went one midnight to consult the stones.

Willie, knowing she was heading there, had got there ahead of her, and with a white sheet folded under his arm he had hidden himself at the edge of the boggy ground to the east of the stone. It was a fine moonlit night, and as Jeannie approached the stone and stood with bowed head, he crept up close. Draping the sheet over his head, he moved towards the stone calling out in an eerie voice, 'Beware, beware, beware. . . .' He had intended saying much else, all about how the young lass was destined to marry a son of the manse and have lots of healthy bairns, and live happily for the rest of her life, but he didn't get to speak another word.

As soon as she saw this strange apparition, Jeannie let out a terrible shriek and took off like a frightened rabbit. Being young and fit she ran like a deer and poor Willie was left standing there, the words fading from his lips as the love of his life ran shrieking into the night. Realising that his plan had

been a miserable failure he sneaked back to the
manse and replaced the white sheet in his mother's
linen chest and went to bed. To bed, but not to
sleep, for he spent the whole night tossing and
turning, his fears about losing Jeannie depriving
him of all but the most fitful sleep.

As it turned out he had every reason to worry.
Jeannie was never sure of what exactly had
happened out there by the stone that night but
once she calmed down she suspected dirty work.
The upshot of it was that she took the words of the
supposed ghost to heart. She decided that she should
beware of Willie, as he was the only one who knew
she had intended going to the stone, and her ardour
soon cooled towards the minister's son. The next
year he could only look sadly on as Jeannie, the
love of his life, got married to the local smith.
And she did live happily the rest of her life and had
a fine brood of healthy and happy children!

the lost coffin

A SIMILAR OCCASION arose when another local
lass couldn't make up her mind between two lads.
One of them was the son of the farmer of Drumgley,
and was considered a pretty good catch. Drumgley
was a wealthy man and in time his son would inherit
a considerable farm as well as a considerable fortune.
Jessie however wasn't sure if she preferred young

Drumgley or Willie Johnston, a local carpenter. Willie was a fine handsome lad, had a steady trade and was well known for his general good humour and good heart. This propensity for laughter was accompanied by a love of a good time, and in those days that could be understood as meaning a liking for strong drink – quite a common situation. Anyway young Jessie had been wooed by the pair of them and just couldn't make up her mind what to do.

Her friends though had no doubt as to what should be done. She should consult the oracle! All the young lassies knew about the supposed power of St Orland's Stone and encouraged her to go to the stone at midnight and ask it to make the right decision for her. Now rural communities in those days were hardly the sorts of places where keeping secrets was easy – particularly if it involved the love lives of young lads and lasses. So when Jessie decided that she would go a certain night to St Orland's stone and lay her problem before it, it didn't take long for the word to spread round the lasses of the district. And both young Drumgley and Willie had sisters of their own, so both of them had the story whispered in their ears that Jessie was going to go one certain night to St Orland's stone and not come back till a decision was made about who she was going to marry.

In these cynical times such faith in an old

superstition might seem a bit quaint, but Jessie was deadly serious. On the decision made that night rested the whole of the rest of her life. However, on the fateful day Willie was called away to the funeral of an elderly uncle at Claypotts, just to the north of Broughty Ferry and a fair few miles from Glamis. As was the way of things, only men went to the funeral and though the service was in Claypotts Kirk, near where Willie's uncle had lived, he had stipulated in his will that he was to be buried beside the rest of his family in Glamis kirk-yard. Willie thought little of this for he was sure that he could attend his uncle's funeral, convey the body back for internment at Glamis and still have plenty of time to be at St Orland's Stone. Both he and Drumgley were aware that the other knew what was going on and feared that if just one of them was nearby the stone that night he would be the one to win Jessie's hand.

Well, the day came and the funeral went well enough and the coffin was put on the back of a farm cart that had been draped in black cloth for the occasion. The cart with the mourners walking behind set off on the twelve or so miles back to Glamis.

The sad cortège passed through the village of Ballumbie and headed north-west to Powrie Brae. Up the brae they went and on past Tealing. Now, it has long been a custom at Scottish funerals for the odd drink to be taken, and by the time they got to

Todhills, where the roads to Forfar and Glamis forked, the funeral party had already passed several taverns. It was generally considered that the time for a drink in honour of Willie's uncle was long overdue! So tethering the horse with its doleful cargo outside the hostelry at Todhills, the party entered the building. A round of drinks was set up and the health of the departed was toasted. Another round was quickly set up and drunk down.

In those days the measures of whisky they were drinking were not like the wee dribbles that pass for a decent drink in hostelries these days. These were real glasses of whisky that they were knocking back! And after a couple more rounds, as the craic began to warm up and stories of the departed were told to increasing hilarity, another Scots habit kicked in. This was the unfortunate habit of buying rounds. If someone buys you a drink, you are obliged to buy that person one back, though sadly there are some dishonourable creatures who are prepared to take advantage of such situations and never put their hands in their pockets, though they are generally despised for their meanness. So the rounds flew and the afternoon passed in an increasingly jolly haze. It was after dark when Willie's father remembered his responsibilities to his brother-in-law and called the party together to complete the journey. So the whole group of them came out – or should I say fell out –

of the tavern at Todhills. And what did they find? Nothing. The horse, the cart and its cargo had disappeared!

Now at any time this would be a dreadful situation, but when everyone in the company is 'roarin' fou', as the poet would describe it, things can be particularly distressful. Some of them fell on their knees and began to moan that it had been stolen by Auld Hornie himself as a punishment from the Lord for their transgressions in getting drunk. Others got angry and were sure that some-one had stolen the horse and cart, while the (slightly) more sober ones reckoned that maybe the horse had just tugged itself free and wandered off. What was clear was that there needed to be a search party. This took a wee while to organise but soon there were drunken mourners heading off up the road to Forfar, some towards Glamis itself, while another group headed back towards Dundee to try and find the lost coffin. In the course of the search there were several accidents due to the darkness of the night and the drunkenness of the searchers, but that is another story for another time.

Suffice it to say that it was more than a few hours later that the horse, cart and coffin were finally located at Glamis Home Farm. The horse had simply got tired of waiting, tugged its halter free and wandered back to its own stable at Glamis, something that led the women of Willie's family to regularly comment that even a farm horse had more sense than their men. Willie was one of the group that located the lost coffin, and such was the all-round relief that they repaired to a nearby house for a celebratory drink, which is quite understandable in the situation. But it was after midnight by this time and it wasn't till the morning that Willie realised what he had done. So a few months later there was nothing he could do but shake young Drumgley by the hand when he married Jessie. He never knew whether to blame himself, the horse, or the drink, but it was noticeable from then on that Willie Johnston, though still a happy and likeable lad, was less to the fore when the time for a dram came round.

battle tales

the Battle of Dunnichen

NE DAMP AUTUMN night in the 1950s a woman was looking out, walking her dog close to the wee village of Dunnichen, near Forfar. She was looking south over an area of farmland around the White Burn, which had been drained the previous century, and had used to be called Dunnichen Moss. It was an area that was well known for becoming waterlogged and boggy in rainy weather. She saw what she thought was a light and looked closer. There seemed to be a group of shadowy figures moving around and holding flaming torches. She rubbed her eyes and looked again.

'What would people be doing down there this late?' she thought. 'And why would they be carrying torches of wood rather than using battery torches?'

Her dog, which had been ahead of her on the road, came back to her and started growling. She bent down to pet the Highland terrier, which seemed a bit upset. She stroked the dog and gently spoke to it till it seemed a bit calmer. As she stood up to head back to the village she glanced again towards the White Burn. There was nothing there. She went home and promptly forgot all about it until a couple of days later when she was talking to her next door neighbour and mentioned what she had seen. Her neighbour stood back a bit gave her a strange look.

'What's wrong?' she asked.

'Ye're sure ye saw fowk wi torches down in the moss?' the neighbour asked.

'Aye, I am,' she replied, puzzled.

Having only been in the village a few years, she had never heard tell of the story that unfolded later that day as, beside Aberlemno Kirk, she listened to her neighbour. They were standing in front of the Pictish Symbol Stone there. On the stones were warriors, on foot and on horseback and pointing to various figures. Her neighbour told her the story the stone commemorated.

It was back in the 680s AD, and the Picts were in deep trouble. Much of their southern lands had been overrun by the Northumbrians and in battle after battle they had been defeated by the Angles. These kings had been expanding their power throughout central and southern Scotland and the north of England for decades, and the blood of Pictish warriors had flowed like rivers trying to fight them off. Not content with taking control of the area up to the Forth, the Northumbrians had pushed north and caused great damage through the lands of the Picts. None of their warriors had been able to stand against the power of Ecgfrith, the current King of Northumbria.

Then the leader of the Pictish peoples died and was replaced by a strong warrior, Brude Mac Bile. Now, like all of the tribesmen of his time, Brude had been raised to be a warrior and was now a man of great strength and undoubted bravery, as well as a man skilled in the use of arms. However, he was more than that. He possessed great intelligence and had a capacity for seeing the big picture – good qualities in a military leader at any time. He was now the leader of the Picts and had nothing in his mind but lifting the yoke of Northumbrian power that was bearing down on his kinsmen and fellow Picts. So he laid his plans to take on the might of the Northumbrian army and defeat them for all time.

Now Ecgfrith and the Northumbrians – in their battles with the Picts, the Scots and the Britons of Strathclyde, as well as other peoples down in England – had been victorious for decades. They could not even conceive of the idea of defeat. In times gone by the Picts had often allied with the Strathclyde Britons and the Scots of Dalriada to fight mutual enemies, but this time Brude was going to settle matters with Pictish warriors only. He provoked a series of confrontations with the Angles in Fife and the Lothians, knowing that in time Ecgfrith himself would come to put down what he considered the unruly and inferior people who were daring to contest his power. Brude was more than ready.

When Ecgfrith at last came north with a great army, Brude's tactic was to lure him on by fighting no more than light skirmishes with small numbers of his warriors – just enough to make the Northumbrians chase after them. So the Northumbrians went deeper and deeper into the Pictish lands. The further they went, the more their supply lines were stretched and the greater the distance from their homeland of Northumbria and their power centres in southern Scotland grew. When battle came, Brude wanted there to be no chance of reinforcements for his enemy.

On and on they went through Fife and up Strathmore, between the Sidlaw Hills and the Grampians. Whenever it looked as though the Northumbrians were going to settle down in one place and harry the surrounding countryside, groups of Brude's men would attack and retreat, drawing the Northumbrians on. Now Ecgfrith had no idea that the Picts had gathered a substantial army – it was only a few years ago that the waters of the River Carron on the south of the Forth had run red with the blood of slain Pictish warriors in a great Northumbrian victory near modern Falkirk. However, Brude had sent word round all the lands of the Picts, far to the north of Scotland and into every glen and strath, summoning warriors to his side.

At last he was ready. The great Northumbrian army, formed of men on horseback and foot, was hot on the heels of a group of Pictish skirmishers as they came through the gap between Lownie Hill and Fotheringham Hill just south of Forfar.

The Pictish skirmishers stuck close to the edge
of Lownie as they ran towards Dunnichen Moss,
then an extensive area of bog. On they ran between
the bog and Dunnichen Hill as the Northumbrian
army came round the edge of the hill behind them.
They kept running till all the Angles had followed
them and were streaming between bog and hill.
Then, at a shouted command, they turned and
stood their ground. The Northumbrians slowed
their pursuit. Now they had their prey and it
would be short work to eradicate this group of no
more than a few hundred men. Then came a great
noise. The Northumbrians turned and looked north
towards the hilltop. There on the top of Dunnichen
Hill was a much larger group of Picts, streaming
down upon them in full battle-charge. Those at the
rear of the Northumbrian army heard another great
shout from behind them. They turned to see yet
another mass of Pictish warriors, who had been
hidden round the edge of Lownie Hill, come
charging towards them.

The battle was hard and many brave Pictish
warriors died that day. But the Northumbrian army
was almost totally wiped out. They were caught
with Pictish warriors on three sides, those ahead of
them having been strengthened by more of their
kinsmen, who had been waiting for their moment.
Many of the Northumbrian warriors were forced
into the great swamp but few escaped through it to

return home and tell their tale. Ecgfrith himself was killed by Brude while trying to flee the battle on a Pictish horse, his own having been killed under him. But his flight was short. This is shown on the battle stone in Aberlemno Kirkyard. After the battle Brude made sure his enemy was given an honourable burial, and then told his men that a famous victory was theirs and that the Picts again were free of foreign domination. And there are those that say it was this great victory that stopped the expansionism of the Northumbrians and laid the basis for the modern country of Scotland. If Ecgfrith had won then he would have assimilated the Picts into his ever-growing state. Brude Mac Bile made sure that never happened.

So nearly fifteen hundred years after that battle on the twentieth of May 685, the story was told again in Aberlemno Kirkyard. And there was no doubt in the minds of the locals that the woman out walking her dog had seen the ghosts of women and other non-combatants searching the field of battle for the bodies of their loved ones who had fallen in the famous victory against the Northumbrian invaders.

scotland's national flag

THROUGHOUT MUCH OF the seventh and eighth
centuries the Picts had been involved in battles with
the expanding kingdom of Northumbria. There had
been bloody affrays in the Lothians and much further
north, including the decisive Battle of Dunnichen.
There is one other battle involving the Picts and
Northumbrians where there is no doubt about the
location, or its importance in Scottish history.

This battle took place much later when once
again the Northumbrians were on the march.
Now when talking about those far off days, when
we say 'kingdoms' we don't mean nation states
with clearly defined borders. Things were much more
fluid back then and, given the essentially tribal
nature of much of British society, it is even likely
that many of the battles we think of as dynastic
were just as much to do with raiding for cattle and
other goods as they were about anything to do
with kingship. Be that as it may, in 832 the
Northumbrians were once again marching north
through the Lothians. The king of the Picts, Angus
– realising that the Northumbrians, under their
own king, Athelstan, were much more numerous
than any army he could put together – had entered
into an alliance with Eochaidh, king of the Scots of
Dalriada. Together they hoped their combined forces
could stop the Southrons in their tracks. Both knew

that if the Northumbrians defeated either one of them it wouldn't be long before the other was in deep trouble.

Although the Picts and Scots had often been at each other's throats over the centuries they were in many cases related and several Scots had actually been kings of the Picts before this. Angus's own father Fergus was probably a Scot, and it is likely that he and Eochaidh saw each other as cousins. As Scotland's history clearly shows, this would not have stopped them fighting each other if they thought it was worth their while, but once again it was clear that the Angles of Northumbria were intent on taking over as much of Britain as they could. Simply to survive, the Picts and Scots had to defeat them together. Both kings were aware that the Northumbrians would have no intention of stopping at the Forth and that the Anglian army would conquer all of Alba if it could. So they decided to launch a preventative raid on the Northumbrian troops that had already begun moving into the Lothians.

The combined armies of the Picts and the Scots marched south-eastward through the Lothians and down into the lands known as the Merse. Initially they met with success and the Northumbrians melted away before them. However it wasn't long before their scouts let them know that a massive army of Angles and Saxons was heading north, led by Athelstan, a famed Northumbrian war-leader.

Given the numbers that were approaching, Angus and Eochaidh had little choice but to retreat northwards.

Angus was certain that he would not be able to turn the tables on Athelstan the way that Brude had tricked Ecgfrith all those generations before. But both men knew there was little choice but to turn and fight at some point or the Northumbrians would simply pursue them deep into their own territories. So they were looking for a suitable ground to fight on when they came to the river Peffer, which runs from near Haddington to the North Sea. In those days before the countryside was drained for modern farming, the Peffer was a much bigger watercourse than it is today and the combined Pictish and Scottish forces decided to stand and fight at a ford across the river not far from East Linton.

The hope was that fighting at the ford would give them some advantage in the coming battle as only limited numbers of Northumbrians would be able to come at them at any one time. The site of the stand was in the area of Markle just to the north of the modern village of Athelstaneford, where the Peffer, which flows into the Firth of Forth at Aberlady, forms a wide valley. The Peffer presented a major obstacle to crossing, and the Picts and Scots camped near the modern farm of Prora – one of the fields there is still known as the Bloody Lands. Scouts were sent out to see where the Northumbrians were. The news that came back was bad, very bad. The much larger force of Northumbrians, with their Saxon allies, was approaching the Picts and Scots from three directions. The situation appeared hopeless. By now it was late and the scouts reckoned that the invaders would be upon them at first light the next day.

Neither Angus nor Eochaidh were cowards. They would pray for guidance and go into battle like true warriors when the Northumbrians came upon them. So Angus led the assembled force in prayers, all of the warriors kneeling in ranks before the two kings. As he finished his prayers Angus looked up into the clear blue sky. There across most of the visible sky was a great sign. It was a massive diagonal cross. Against the blue of the sky it could hardly be clearer.

'What is this sign!' he exclaimed.

At that, one of the monks accompanying the armies came forward and said, 'That, Angus, is the shape of the cross on which the Blessed St Andrew, brother of the great St Peter, was martyred. I think he has sent us a sign.'

'If this be true,' said Angus, rising to his feet and drawing his sword, 'it is perhaps then a sign of our victory and I will pledge this here and now. If we win the victory against these marauding Northumbrians tomorrow, we shall take this sign as a flag and we will make St Andrew our patron saint.'

The warriors nearby heard what the king had said and whispers spread throughout the ranks. There had been a sign from a great Christian martyr. Surely it meant that victory was assured. They all began to rise and look at the sky above. Realising that the sign was visible to all, Angus turned and whispered to Eochaidh. Both then raised their swords and addressed their warriors in their own tongues, telling them of this great omen of victory that had come to them.

The next day the Northumbrian army came on the Picts and Scots, and the battle was hard. Just when it seemed that all would be lost, once again the white cross appeared in the sky and the warriors of Angus and Eochaidh fought with renewed vigour, even as the symbol caused fear and consternation amongst the Southron forces. The fighting was at its wildest and bloodiest at the crossing of the Peffer Burn, where Athelstan himself fell, fighting like a true warrior to the very last. It was afterwards given the name of Athelstaneford because of his bravery.

When the battle was done at last, and Angus and Eochaidh met amongst the piled corpses of the slain, both were convinced that divine intervention had helped them win this great victory, even if it had cost them dearly in the number of fallen warriors. Friends and relatives lay dead around the battlefield. But the rump of the Northumbrians was heading back south and the great Athelstan had been defeated.

Within fifty years of this victory the Picts and the Scots were finally united under Kenneth MacAlpine. Following the vows made by his predecessors, he was pleased to declare St Andrew the patron saint of the new united country, and adopted as the national flag the white diagonal cross against a sky blue background. This symbol, that had so inspired the warriors of the Picts and Scots on that distant day in the Lothians, when it appeared in the sky to promise a remarkable victory, we continue to hold dear as the Saltire.

Death of a Hero

Strathardle is the name given to the valley formed by the river of the same name, which runs north-wards from the Bridge of Cally into the hills of Blairgowrie, and onto the Moulin moors east of Pitlochry. A couple of miles to the north of Kirkmichael, the village in the strath, is the wee hamlet of Enochdu. Here, by the side of the road, is a burial mound, still clearly visible, that is marked on the maps as the Giant's Grave.

It was in the ancient times when the Galls – the name for the Viking-like ancestors of the modern Norwegians and Danes – were regularly raiding the lands of the Picts. There were two kinds of invaders in those dark days, the *Dubh-Gall*, the dark strangers, who came from the land we call Norway,

and the *Fionn-Gall*, the fair strangers, who came
from Denmark and the areas to the south. They had
started by raiding the coasts but soon they were
driving deep into the straths and glens of Scotland,
slaughtering as they went and lifting everything of
value they could lay their hands on. Although starting
out as little more than raiders, the marauding
northern warriors seemed close to taking control of
the whole of Scotland.

Time after time the Picts, and their cousins the
Scots, had met the Galls in battle, and time after
time they had been defeated. Now a great army of
Galls had come up the Strathtay and over the
Moulin moors. Those who managed to escape the
army were fleeing ever deeper into the hills. The
invaders knew that the local people kept their herds
of cattle up in high pastures throughout the summer,
and it seemed likely they wanted to round up all
the cows in the area. There were several thousand
of these *Fionn-Gall* and they had a great longing
for fresh beef, so they headed into the hills. Up
ahead of them, however, a large force of Picts was
waiting. These were under the leadership of Ard-
fhuil, a high-born warrior said to be the son of
Cruithne, the first of all the Picts. Ard-fhuil had
fought the raiders many times and been forced to
retreat, but now he had gathered up many
scattered bands of Pictish warriors and had made
his mind up that it was time for victory. They were

waiting hidden behind the hill of An Tulach as the Norsemen came south down the glen, watched all the way by the Picts. At last the Galls were strung out along the glen floor and Ard-fhuil gave the order to charge. Down the side of the hill poured the Pictish army, using the lie of the land just as their descendants in the Highland clans were still doing a thousand years later.

The first the Norsemen knew of the ambush was when they heard the war cries of the Picts as they fell upon them. In the initial charge hundreds of the Norsemen died. Yet they too were battle hardened warriors and they managed to rally together. The Picts fought as if mad and, bit by bit, began to drive the invaders back. And at the head of the Pictish thrust was Ard-fhuil himself, cutting down Norse warriors one after another. Given the fierceness of this assault it was but a matter of time before the Norsemen's re-formed line broke and at a cry from one of their leaders, they turned and ran back up the glen. A great shout of triumph went up from the Picts, many of whom rested on their swords as they watched the Norsemen flee.

But not Ard-fhuil. He was in the full-blooded heat of battle and would not be happy till the last of these vile incomers lay dead before him. So he hared after the fleeing warriors. With him went just one of his cousins, for his bodyguard, made up of his closest kinfolk, was scattered over the battlefield

and, with more than a few of their number
littering the valley behind them, the rest did not see
what was happening. On the Norsemen ran, looking
over their shoulders. At their rear was an old and
crafty warrior who noticed that there were but two
Picts following them. Just as they came to Enochdhu
and forded the churning waters of Allt Doire nan
Eun – the Burn of the Birds – which flows down
from the hills to the east, the old Norseman gave a
shout. All at once about twenty of the fleeing
Norsemen turned and ran back at Ard-fhuil and
his cousin.

The odds were far too great and within a
minute or two, the Picts lay dead on the ground.
The Norsemen turned and ran off northward again.
It was only a couple of minutes before the rest of
Ard-fhuil's closest kin came hurrying after him but
they were too late. Their leader, the one who had
planned and executed this great victory over the
Norse invaders, lay dead in the grass. He had died
a hero's death but the pleasure of the victory went
sour for his relatives and many another Pict.
Quickly a large group was organised to chase after
the fleeing Norsemen and hunt them down.

Many more men died that day but by its end
the invading Norsemen had been driven back,
never to show their faces in the glens of Perthshire
again. Then Ard-fhuil, son of Cruithne, was laid to
rest by his kin, with all due ceremony, below the

burial mound they now call the Giant's Grave. And ever since then the river and the strath it runs through have carried the name of the great and victorious leader of the Picts who gave his life in clearing the land of invaders. Which is why to this day we call it Strathardle.

the Battle of Blath Bhalg

BUT THIS STORY of battle is not the only one in Strathardle. Today it is a peaceful place with farms, hunting estates and an environmental centre attracting many visitors, but it has a bloody past. For high on the western slopes of Strathardle, more than half a century before the Vikings came, Pictish warriors spilt the blood of their fellow Picts and kinsmen. The Picts were a race of warriors, so when a leader or king died, his succession was not always peaceful. Since time immemorial there had been a considerable element of election in the choosing of the Pictish high-chief, a position akin to what we now call king. The best man of all those in the line of succession was the preferred option, and the tribesmen hoped they would know which of the candidates would be the most fitted. As the Picts claimed their right through their mother's kin it wasn't just a matter of choosing one from amongst brothers. There could be uncles, as well as brothers and nephews of the last monarch. The

candidate would not just have to be an able
warrior – all of them were that – he would need
to be able to judge his own kin, be capable of
tempering justice with mercy, yet able to strike
quickly and without doubt when the situation arose.
Just as the later clansmen picked the ablest warrior
of their kin to lead them in battle, the leading kin-
groups of the Picts had the right to select who was
to have leadership over all of them. Yet it is the
way of human nature that not everyone can agree.
And there are always those whose ambition runs
ahead of their ability.

So it happened in the early years of the eighth
century that Nechtan son of Derile renounced the
leadership of the Picts and went off to live the
quiet contemplative life of a monk in a monastery.
The details are unclear but there are those who will
tell you that he did not do this lightly or even of
his own accord. Now it was time for a new leader
to be found. There were four contenders, Angus
son of Fergus, the brothers Drest and Alpin and
their cousin, another Nechtan. There was a series
of battles between them. And one of these, it is
said, took place in Strathardle.

This was a battle between Drest and Angus and
it was fought on the hill of Blath Bhalg at the head
of Glen Derby, which runs west into the hills from
just below Kirkmichael. In those far off times it
was the custom for the bards to rouse the warriors

to battle, reminding them of the great bravery and overwhelming victories of their noble ancestors. The two opposing forces were drawn up opposite each other on the southeast slope of Blath Bhalg. The bard of the Southern Picts, the men of Fortriu led by Angus, stood before the assembled host and incited them on to victory.

'Take courage my brothers, for even though it is against our cousins we must fight this day, fear not, for I have had a vision and I tell you this: That by this day's end Angus, our leader, will win victory for us all,' he cried out to resounding cheers. And brave warrior that he was, he took his spear in hand and rushed headlong at the enemy, followed by the men of Fortriu. The battle then raged all along the eastern slopes of the mountain. In the bloody carnage that took place that day – for when relatives fight, rarely is mercy shown – the very first man to fall was the brave bard. But his words were prophetic and Angus and his men of Fortriu won the day, Drust and the scattered remnants of his kin fleeing off to the north-west.

After the battle the men gathered to give honour to their bard, and they buried him there in a hollow on the hillside that to this day still carries the name Corrie a' Bhaird, the Bard's Corrie. Then the bodies of the fallen were gathered up, and there were so many of them that taking them off for burial at home was impossible. So the dead

from both sides were gathered up and cast into the
lochan, or small loch, above Corrie a' Bhaird.
They fought each other in life but were together in
death. Even this day those still waters carry the
name Lochan Dubh, the Dark Lochan or Tarn, not
for its dark waters, but for the deep sorrow in the
hearts of the surviving warriors as they said
farewell to the Picts slain in battle that day above
Strathardle. It is a place few locals have visited
over the years for it is considered to be haunted by
the sad spirits of those who fell in that battle, Pict
against Pict.

war of the dog

BACK IN THE time of the Picts, some of their kings
were chosen from amongst neighbouring peoples, like
the Scots. It is said that this was because the right to
the kingship came from marrying the queen of the
Picts and it meant that while sometimes the Picts were
at war with their neighbours, at other times they were
at peace with them. It was in one of these periods of
peace that a king of the Scots, called Crathinluth,
invited a band of young Pictish warriors to come and
stay at his capital of Dunadd in the Kilmartin valley.
The Scots, just like the Picts at the time, were a tribal
warrior society and the chiefs tended to have a group
of young warriors with them at all times. It was the
accepted thing for young men to spend a period in

their late teens as full-time warriors before settling down to married life within the community, and this had the added benefit of keeping troublesome adolescents busy. Young men have always had a tendency towards what you can call 'unfocussed behaviour', like mischief and just plain trouble. However, it was a great compliment to this particular band of young Picts to be asked to go and be part of Crathinluth's household, and of course the wiser heads amongst both peoples thought it was a good idea that would help to keep the current peace between them. But young men are prone to rash acts that, while they might start off as mischief, can quickly develop into something much more serious.

This band of Picts had been out with Crathinluth, hunting boar in the forests to the north of the Kilmartin valley, and a couple of them had noticed how fond he was of one particular brown and white hunting hound. One night, after drinking deep of their favourite drink, heather yill, which they had the unfortunate foresight to bring plenty of, they decided to play a trick on their host by taking his favourite hound and hiding it. They were successful in stealing the dog and hiding it in the edge of a wood near where they themselves were camping out. However, Crathinluth's hounds were under the charge of a very experienced old warrior and he soon figured out what had happened.

He managed to track the dog to where it was

hidden and was just about to take it back when a handful of the young Picts came upon him. Words were exchanged, tempers rose, swords were drawn and things quickly went from bad to worse. Fired up with drink, and upset that the trick had been found out, one of the Picts made as if to attack the old warrior. At this the dog, which had been quiet up till now, went for him. Unthinkingly he stabbed the dog through the heart. The dog's guardian lunged at him and was struck down by his companions! Their mischief had indeed gone bad. Both the king's favourite hound and its keeper lay dead on the ground.

Realising the utter stupidity of their actions, the youths ran back to tell the rest of their comrades what had happened. There was little option. If they went to Crathinluth and admitted to what they had done, those that had spilt the old warrior's blood were likely to lose their lives. There were only one or two older and more experienced warriors amongst them and they agreed the only way out of the mess was to head back to the east as quickly as possible and try to come to an arrangement later. They hoped they would be able to make some sort of money settlement for the old man's life. So, under cover of darkness the entire contingent of Picts slipped off through the forest and headed over Drumalbain. They left no one to tell their side of the story – a sad and costly mistake.

The following morning Crathinluth was told that the Picts had killed both his trusted Master of Hounds and his favourite hound and then slipped off under cover of darkness. This was a dreadful insult and at once he sent off a hand-picked band of experienced warriors to hunt them down. When they returned three days later, they reported that the Picts had managed to elude them after a short skirmish and returned home. However, in the fighting a couple of warriors from both sides had been killed. At once Crathinluth sent word to the Pictish court that the perpetrators were to be handed over, or else. As soon as the messenger was sent, Crathinluth began raising an army. Fine well he knew that if he wanted justice, he might well have to fight for it.

Back in Pictland, having told their sorry tale, the young band stressed that the pursuing Scots had killed two of their number. When the peremptory demand to hand the culprits over came from the Scots, there were a few voices that urged calm and an attempt to negotiate. However, many of the Pictish warriors saw Crathinluth's demand as an insult in itself and were all for defending their own. So the Pictish chiefs had little choice but to call together their own warriors and the scene was set for a battle. Neither side was prepared to give way and the pleas for peace from wiser heads on both sides were ignored. Conflict was now inevitable

and over the next couple of weeks small battles
started to erupt through the border country between
the two peoples. In these small battles more warriors
lost their lives, stoking further resentment.

Things just got worse from there. The battles that
were fought gradually involved greater numbers, and
the numbers of the slain on each side continued to
rise. Both peoples were composed of warrior tribes
and neither would ever think of giving way – their
honour demanded victory. The peace that had
existed before was forgotten and the slaughter and
enmity grew. It seemed as if the war would continue
till one side proved totally triumphant or all the
warriors on both sides were dead!

The wiser, older men and women who realised
the stupidity of the war were at their wits' end.
They knew that they could only bring the fighting
warriors to their senses by finding someone both
sides could respect, that they both might listen to.
But with the whole country in arms, and all the
tribes on one side or another, who could they call
on? It was then that a strange thing happened.
One of the elder Picts, an adviser to the queen,
suggested a warrior that had the respect of both
sides. Both sides had fought with this man and had
respect for him. At last a possible candidate for
referee was found. So word was sent south, to the
great fort on the mighty wall the Roman legions
had built from the Tyne to the Solway. There a

message was given to Carausius, the famous
Roman who had come over from Armorica on the
continent to defend the wall. Here was someone
who had the respect of both Scots and Picts, even if
both sides would be happy to see the back of him
and all his foreign troops!

Carausius was astounded. These barbarians, as
the Romans saw them, were attacking each other
and making his life easier. While they were distracted
they would not be harrying his troops. However,
although he had been a soldier many years, and
had taken part in many brutal campaigns for the
Roman Senate, in his heart he was a fair and honest
man. He told the Pictish messengers he would
think abut what they proposed and let them know
within a few days. Though it caused him several
sleepless nights this veteran Roman at last decided
that he would try to do what he was asked, and
sent word to the leaders of both peoples.

Astounded at this intervention both
Crathinluth and his opposite number, Drest, agreed
to meet with the Roman on neutral ground far to
the south, near the wall itself. And here under the
careful diplomacy of Carausius the two peoples
were persuaded of the folly of carrying on the
fighting. It was only at this fateful meeting that
Crathinluth heard what had actually happened and
on considering the cost of what had surely been
little more than stupidity on the part of the young

Pictish band, he agreed that talk of peace was desirable.

And so it was that the Picts and Scots, with the help of a Roman general, put aside their ill feelings and once more entered into a period of peace. A period of peace that ended with them allying themselves against the Romans, as they had done so often before!

and finally . . .

hamlet and the queen of the picts

NOW SHAKESPEARE'S VERSION of the old Scandinavian story of Hamlet is very well known, but he didn't tell the half of it. What we know is that the story is very old and, from what we can tell, one of the protagonists seems to have been the queen of the Picts, Haermdrude by name. The old idea that the sovereignty of the Picts was passed down the female line is one that has received a lot of support recently. Though the story contains references to kingdoms like England, Denmark and Scotland, it seems likely that the tale is describing events that could have happened before these kingdoms took on anything like their modern size or shape. As we have the story, Hamlet, just as Shakespeare tells us, was sent to England with a secret message from his father-in-law to have him killed. Hamlet, despite what problems he may have had, was a very intelligent young man and managed to avoid this planned fate, going so far as to turn the tables on his supposed assassins, and ending up marrying the king of England's daughter before returning to Denmark. After he returned to Denmark he avenged his father's death by killing his uncle and stepfather, who in this version is called Fenge.

After this he took on the position of king of Denmark before returning to England to see his wife and father-in-law.

Now the king of England had been a friend of Fenge's when they were young men and, as warriors often did in those olden times, they had sworn to avenge each other if either of them was unfairly killed. The king of England hadn't got the original message from Fenge when Hamlet first came to England and had no idea how things were playing out in Denmark. When his son-in-law returned he was anxious to get news of his old friend and was in fact extremely shocked to hear that Hamlet had killed his stepfather and taken his throne. At the same time the king of England could hardly avenge Fenge publicly – not only would he be breaking all known rules of hospitality but, by killing the current king of Denmark, he might provoke war. So, keeping a straight face, he told Hamlet that he understood that he had had no choice but to avenge his father's death, and asked him to stay for a while at his stronghold in England. This was to give himself time to devise a plan, for he had no intention of doing anything other than fulfilling his ancient vow to Fenge, though he couldn't be seen to be doing it.

It just so happened that the queen of England had died just the year before and the king was on the lookout for a new wife. She had to be someone of suitable standing, he explained to Hamlet, and told

him that he had decided that he wanted to marry
the queen of the Picts. At this Hamlet was aghast.

'But father,' he said, 'You know what is said of
her. Not a single suitor that has approached her
has been allowed to live. She has killed them all.
Isn't it said that she hates men and has no intention
of ever allowing one into her bed?'

'Ah yes, my son,' the king replied with a smile.
'I know that they say this but she is a queen and if
someone of suitable rank approaches her she will
remember her position and all will be well. That is
why I want you, my own dear son-in-law, to take this
letter to her and ask for her hand in marriage on my
behalf.' At this he smiled a gentle, loving smile and
put his hand on Hamlet's shoulder. Hamlet's blood
ran cold. This was a dangerous mission indeed.
However he thought that the king, older and wise in
the ways of men and women, was perhaps right and
that the queen would look kindly on him.

Hamlet had no idea of just how dangerous
things were. The letter the king gave him did ask for
the queen of the Picts' hand in marriage but it went
much farther. It promised great riches if the queen
would dispose of the messenger and all his companions. Unaware of all this Hamlet set off for the far
north with a group of his own close companions and
a small number of the king of England's men. The
king had no compunction about sending these men
to their deaths, just as long as his vow was filled.

So the group set off towards Scotland. In those
far off days travelling across country was slow
– there were few roads better than forest tracks
and in many places there were great dense woods
interspersed with long tracts of boggy ground, all
of which took time to cross. At last, however, they
got north of the Forth and, having travelled much
of the night, they stopped in a small clearing in
the forest below an overhanging rock. It was a
beautiful spot with a bright burn running through
it, and once they had drunk their fill they all ate and,
setting guards, Hamlet and his close companions
went to sleep. Now maybe it was just the hot day
and the delightful surroundings, or maybe it was
something to do with the rumoured powers of the
queen of the Picts, but pretty soon virtually the
whole company was sound asleep. As they slept
there in the forest a small hand-picked band of
Pictish warriors crept up on them. Haermdrude
had heard of the approach of a group of men, led
by one who was clearly a man of considerable
importance, and she had sent out her spies.

It so happens that Hamlet was sleeping with his
head resting on his shield, not an uncommon practice
amongst travelling warriors, many of whom would
sleep with their swords in their hands (which had
caused more than a few accidents, but that is
another tale). And Hamlet's shield was unique.
On it he had instructed a great artisan to tell the

story of how he had tricked Fenge and revenged
himself on his father's murderer. Not everybody
would be able to understand the whole story but it
was obviously an important clue as to who this
prince was.

So one of the Picts carefully and skilfully passed
the few of Hamlet's guards who had remained awake
and crept right up to the famous Dane. Slowly and
carefully he removed the shield from under the
sleeping man's head and, remembering what the
queen had told him, he looked into the large bag
lying beside the sleeping warrior. Sure enough there
was a letter signed with an ornate seal and clearly
intended for the queen herself. So, just as slowly
and just as carefully, he pulled the letter from the
bag and made his way through the undergrowth
and back into the forest, dragging the shield behind
him with the letter firmly stowed away inside his
leather coat. As soon as he was well clear he picked
up the shield and ran as fast as he could through the
forest to a nearby clearing. Here the queen herself
was waiting. Like many of her ancestors she
thought of herself as a warrior and was as brave as
any man. She was also, like many of the wisest of
the Picts, both women and men, adept at reading
signs, and once she had read the king's letter she
looked long and hard at the shield.

Now the king of England had said in his letter
that this man was little better than a murderer but

she realised that no one with that character would ever display his actions on his own shield for those who had the knowledge to read it. The idea of marrying the king of England, who was old enough to be her father, held absolutely no attraction for her but she was impressed by what she had read from the shield. This man was quick-witted and brave and from the reports she had received he was good-looking, strong and healthy. For a while now she had been wondering if it was time to take herself a husband. Many of her elderly relatives had been suggesting as much and she knew that amongst the tribes and in her court it was thought time she brought the Picts a new king. So she decided to play a trick on the quick-witted man and see what happened. If things didn't work out, she thought, she could always kill him and his companions later.

Accordingly she sat and composed a letter that looked just like the one the king of England had sent and, carefully, she managed to put the seal back on the letter so it didn't look as if it had been disturbed at all. She then gave it back to the skilful warrior who had got hold of the shield in the first place and told him to take it back and replace it and the letter, just as he had found them. While all this was going on, Hamlet had wakened and realised at once that somebody had gone off with his shield. Reckoning that whoever this joker was, he was quite likely to come back, the wily Dane lay

down again as if asleep. When the Pict crept up
through the bushes with the shield and the letter,
Hamlet was ready and pounced on the scout, calling
for his men for assistance. Within a couple of
minutes the sorry Pict was trussed up like a
chicken. Hamlet retrieved his shield and the king's
letter, had the Pict unceremoniously thrown over
the back of the horse and headed on towards the
queen's stronghold.

Despite the travelling party turning up with a
captured Pict, the queen, who had ridden on ahead
of Hamlet's party, welcomed them graciously.
She took the king's letter and pretended to read it.
After a while she looked up and said, 'Well, King
Hamlet, it seems that you are to be congratulated.
You have avoided some treacherous plans and I
think it fair to say your uncle received his just
desserts.' She went on in a similar vein, making it
quite clear that she thought he was a remarkable
man and, in fact, quite brilliant. She paused to look
at him, then said with a smile, 'The only thing that
trouble me, my Lord, is how you have come to make
such a dire mistake with your marriage.'

At this Hamlet looked puzzled. What was this
imperious, and incidentally very handsome, queen
talking about?

'I think you have married well below
yourself,' the queen went on. 'I take it you are
unaware of the fact that the current king of

England has no real claim to the throne and is in fact common-born?'

Hamlet was forced to admit that he didn't know and was feeling pretty puzzled. He had come here to plead for his father-in-law and here was the queen of the Picts talking about him. What was going on?

'You know,' she continued, 'a wise man should always look beyond beauty in a wife. Looks are not that important and after all they fade with time. It is character and decent birth that make a fitting wife. And I think we have someone who is both your match in noble lineage and riches, and would be an equal partner for you, someone to whom you would not be superior either in royal power or authority. It has long been the habit of my people to have our queens choose who will be the king to lead us and, if you are up to it, why do you not marry me? You can keep that other silly girl as well, she is no threat to me.'

Despite himself, Hamlet was attracted to this idea. After all, everything she said was true and, despite her disparaging remarks about womens' looks, she was herself beautiful, and by marrying her he would be the king of two kingdoms. He also realised that with the power of the Picts and his own warriors from over the sea he would have little to fear from the king of England. It didn't take long for him to accept the sense of what she was saying and a mighty nuptial feast was arranged to happen within a couple of weeks, with people coming from all over Scotland and Scandinavia for the wedding. Down in England the king was not pleased, but realised he had been outfoxed by both of the young people. When Hamlet and Haermdrude came down to visit him, with a large army at their backs, he made them very welcome indeed. And as is often said, treachery is its own reward, for not long after this the king of England was slain himself in very suspicious circumstances by some warriors from Scandinavia, with whom it was said he was plotting yet another attempt on Hamlet's life. And after that Hamlet returned to Denmark with both his wives.

The story, as it comes to us, was told by a monk, who took great pleasure in telling us that when Hamlet knew his time was coming – there was a battle ahead that he could not win – he told Haermdrude to take another man, but she swore to die beside him in battle. The story then goes that rather than do this she stayed behind and married the man who slew him. Decide for yourself if this sounds like the actions of a Pictish queen, but remember what monks were taught to think of women!

BIBLIOGRAphy

Adomnan, *Life of St Columba*. London, 1995.

Barnett, T. R. *Border By-Ways and Lothian Lore*. Edinburgh, 1950.

Bower, W., edited by Watt, D. E. R. *Scotichronicon*, 9 Vols. Aberdeen, 1989.

Buchanan, G. *The History of Scotland*, 5 Vols. Glasgow, 1827.

County Folklore Series: *Fife*. London, 1914.

Dixon, J. *Pitlochry Past and Present*. Pitlochry, 1925.

Douglas, R. M. *The Scots Book*. Edinburgh, 1949.

Fittis, R. S. *Illustrations of Perthshire History*. Perth, 1874.
Historical and traditionary gleanings regarding Perthshire. Perth, 1879.

Guthrie, J. *The Vale of Strathmore, Its Scenes and Legends*. Edinburgh, 1875.

Mackinlay, J. *The Folk Lore of Scottish Lochs and Springs*. Glasgow, 1893.

Ritchie, J. B. *The Pageant of Morayland*. Elgin, 1932.

Small, A. *Some Interesting Roman Antiquities recently discovered in Fife*. Edinburgh, 1823.

Swire, O. *The Highlands and their Legends*. Edinburgh, 1963.

Warden, A. J. *Angus, or Forfarshire*, 5 Vols. Dundee, 1880-1885.

Wilkie, J. *The History of Fife*. Edinburgh, 1924.

Some other books published by **LUATH** PRESS

On the Trail of Scotland's Myths and Legends
Stuart McHardy
ISBN 1 84282 049 4 PB £7.99

Scotland is an ancient land with an extensive heritage of myths and legends that have been passed down by word-of-mouth over the centuries. As the art of storytelling bursts into new flower, many of these tales are being told again as they once were. As *On the Trail of Scotland's Myths and Legends* unfolds, mythical animals, supernatural beings, heroes, giants and goddesses come alive and walk Scotland's rich landscape as they did in the time of the Scots, Gaelic and Norse speakers of the past.

Visiting over 170 sites across Scotland, Stuart McHardy traces the lore of our ancestors, connecting ancient beliefs with traditions still alive today. Presenting a new picture of who the Scottish are and where they have come from these stories provide an insight into a unique tradition of myth, legend and folklore that has marked the language and landscape of Scotland.

... a remarkably keen collection of tales.
NEIL MACARA BROWN, SCOTTISH BOOK COLLECTOR

[Stuart McHardy is] passionate about the place of indigenous culture in Scottish national life.
COURIER AND ADVERTISER

The Quest for the Nine Maidens
Stuart McHardy
ISBN 0 946487 66 9 HB £16.99

When Arthur was conveyed to Avalon they were there. When Odin summoned warriors to Valhalla they were there. When the Greek god Apollo was worshipped on mountaintops they were there. When Brendan came to the Island of Women they were there. Cerridwen's cauldron of inspiration was tended by them and Peredur received his arms from them. They are found in Pictland, Wales, Ireland, Iceland, Gaul, Greece, Africa and possibly as far afield as South America and Oceania.

They are the Nine Maidens, pagan priestesses involved in the worship of the Mother Goddess. From Stone Age rituals to the 20th century, the Nine Maidens come in many forms. Muses, Maenads, valkyries and druidesses all associated with a single male. Weather – workers, shape – shifters, diviners and healers, the Nine Maidens are linked to the Old Religion over much of our planet. In this book Stuart McHardy has traced similar groups of Nine Maidens, throughout the ancient Celtic and Germanic world and far beyond, from Christian and pagan sources. In his search he begins to uncover one of the most ancient and widespread institutions of human society.

The Quest for Arthur
Stuart McHardy
ISBN 1 84282 012 5 HB £16.99

King Arthur of Camelot and the Knights of the Round Table are enduring romantic figures. A national hero for the Bretons, the Welsh and the English alike Arthur is a potent figure for many. This quest leads to a radical new interpretation of the ancient myth.

Historian, storyteller and folklorist Stuart McHardy believes he has uncovered the origins of this inspirational figure, the true Arthur. He incorporates knowledge of folklore and placename studies with an archaeological understanding of the 6th century.

Combining knowledge of the earliest records and histories of Arthur with an awareness of the importance of oral trad tions, this quest leads to the discovery that the enigmatic origins of Arthur lie not in Brittany or England or Wales. Instead they lie in that magic land the ancient Welsh called *Y Gogledd*, the North; the North of Britain which we now call Scotland.

Edinburgh and Leith Pub Guide

Stuart McHardy

ISBN 0 946487 80 4 PB £4.95

You might be in Edinburgh to explore the closes and wynds of one of Europe's most beautiful cities, to sample the finest Scotch whiskies and to discover a rich Celtic heritage of traditional music and storytelling. Or you might be in Leith to get blootered. Either way, this is the guide for you.

Stuart McHardy has dragged his tired old frame around over two hundred pubs – all in the name of research, of course. Alongside drinking numerous pints, he has managed to compile enough historical anecdotes and practical information to allow anyone with a sturdy liver to follow in his footsteps.

Although Stuart unashamedly gives top marks to his favourite haunts, he rates most highly those pubs that are original, distinctive and cater to the needs of their clientele. Be it domino league or play-station league, pina colada or a pint of heavy, filled foccacia or mince and tatties, Stuart has found a decent pub that does it.

Scots Poems to be Read Aloud

Collectit an wi an innin by
Stuart McHardy

ISBN 0 946487 81 2 PBK £5.00

This is a book to encourage the traditional Scottish ceilidh of song and recitation. This personal collection of well-known and not-so-well-known Scots poems to read aloud includes great works of art and

simple pieces of questionable 'literary merit'. For those who love poetry it's a wonderful anthology to have to hand, and for all those people who do not normally read poetry this collection is for you.

Scots Poems to be Read Aloud is pure entertainment – at home, on a stag or a hen night, Hogmanay, Burns Night, in fact any party night.

SUNDAY POST

Luath Storyteller: Highland Myths & Legends

George W. Macpherson

ISBN 1 84282 003 6 PBK £5.99

The mythical, the legendary, the true... This is the stuff of stories and storytellers, the stuff of an age-old tradition in almost every country in the world, and none more so than Scotland. Celtic heroes, Fairies, Druids, Selkies, Sea horses, Magicians, Giants, Viking invaders; all feature in this collection of traditional Scottish tales, the like of which were told round camp fires centuries ago, and are still told today.

George W. Macpherson has dipped into his phenomenal repertoire of tales to compile this diverse collection of traditional stories, designed to be read aloud. Each has been passed from generation to generation, some are two and a half thousand years old.

From the Celtic legends of Cuchullin and Fionn to the mythical tales of seal-people and magicians these stories have a timeless quality. Often, strands of the stories will interweave and cross over, building a delicate tapestry of Scotland as a mystical, enchanted land.

The result is vivid and impressive, conveying the tragic dignity of the ancient warrior, or the devoted love of the seal woman and her

fisher mate. The personalities and circumstances of people long gone are brought fully to life by the power of the storyteller's words. The ancestors take form before us in the visual imagination.
DR DONALD SMITH, THE SCOTTISH STORYTELLING CENTRE

one of Scotland's best storytellers
WESTDEUTSCHER RUNDFUNK KOHN

This is your genuine article
MARK FISHER, THE LIST

Legend and myth join with humour and gentle wit to create a special magic
JOY HENDRY, SCOTSMAN

The Supernatural Highlands
Francis Thompson
ISBN 0 946487 31 6 PBK £8.99

An authoritative exploration of the otherworld of the Highlander, happenings and beings hitherto thought to be outwith the ordinary forces of nature. A simple introduction to the way of life of rural Highland and Island communities, this new edition weaves a path through second sight, the evil eye, witchcraft, ghosts, fairies and other supernatural beings, offering new sightlines on areas of belief once dismissed as folklore and superstition.

This well-researched little book is written by someone who takes very seriously the ancient continuity of Gaelic culture, and asks us to keep an open mind about second sight, or the power of magic.
SCOTLAND ON SUNDAY

The Supernatural Highlands is a substantive and thoughtful book and as such a valuable addition to the popular history of Scotland.
THIS SCOTLAND

FOLKLORE

Tall Tales from an Island
Peter Macnab
ISBN 0 946487 07 3 PB £8.99

Tales of the North Coast
Alan Temperley
ISBN 0 946487 18 9 PB £8.99

THE QUEST FOR

The Quest for the Celtic Key
Karen Ralls-MacLeod and Ian Robertson
ISBN 1 84282 084 2 PB £7.99

The Quest for Charles Rennie Mackintosh
John Cairney
ISBN 1 84282 058 3 HB £16.99

The Quest for Robert Louis Stevenson
John Cairney
ISBN 0 946487 87 1 HB £16.99

The Quest for the Original Horse Whisperers
Russell Lyon
ISBN 1 84282 020 6 HB £16.99

ON THE TRAIL OF

On the Trail of the Pilgrim Fathers
J. Keith Cheetham
ISBN 0 946487 83 9 PB £7.99

On the Trail of Mary Queen of Scots
J. Keith Cheetham
ISBN 0 946487 50 2 PB £7.99

On the Trail of John Wesley
J. Keith Cheetham
ISBN 1 84282 023 0 PB £7.99

On the Trail of William Wallace
David R. Ross
ISBN 0 946487 47 2 PB £7.99

On the Trail of Robert the Bruce
David R. Ross
ISBN 0 946487 52 9 PB £7.99

On the Trail of Robert Service
GW Lockhart
ISBN 0 946487 24 3 PB £7.99

On the Trail of John Muir
Cherry Good
ISBN 0 946487 62 6 PB £7.99

On the Trail of Robert Burns
John Cairney
ISBN 0 946487 51 0 PB £7.99

On the Trail of Bonnie Prince Charlie
David R Ross
ISBN 0 946487 68 5 PB £7.99

On the Trail of Queen Victoria in the Highlands
Ian R Mitchell
ISBN 0 946487 79 0 PB £7.99

ISLANDS

The Islands that Roofed the World: Easdale, Belnahua, Luing & Seil:
Mary Withall
ISBN 0 946487 76 6 PB £4.99

Rum: Nature's Island
Magnus Magnusson
ISBN 0 946487 32 4 PB £7.95

LUATH GUIDES TO SCOTLAND

The North West Highlands: Roads to the Isles
Tom Atkinson
ISBN 1 84282 086 9 PB £5.99

Mull and Iona: Highways and Byways
Peter Macnab
ISBN 1 84282 089 3 PB £5.99

The Northern Highlands: The Empty Lands
Tom Atkinson
ISBN 1 84282 087 7 PB £5.99

The West Highlands: The Lonely Lands
Tom Atkinson
ISBN 1 84282 088 5 PB £5.99

LANGUAGE

Luath Scots Language Learner [Book]
L Colin Wilson
ISBN 0 946487 91 X PB £9.99

Luath Scots Language Learner [Double Audio CD Set]
L Colin Wilson
ISBN 1 84282 026 5 CD £16.99

GENEALOGY

Scottish Roots: step-by-step guide for ancestor hunters
Alwyn James
SBN 1 84282 090 7 PB £6.99

WALK WITH LUATH

Skye 360: walking the coastline of Skye
Andrew Dempster
SBN 0 946487 85 5 PB £8.99

Walks in the Cairngorms
Ernest Cross
SBN 0 946487 09 X PB £4.95

Short Walks in the Cairngorms
Ernest Cross
ISBN 0 946487 23 5 PB £4.95

The Joy of Hillwalking
Ralph Storer
ISBN 1 84282 069 9 PB £7.50

Scotland's Mountains before the Mountaineers
Ian R Mitchell
ISBN 0 946487 39 1 PB £9.99

Mountain Days & Bothy Nights
Dave Brown & Ian R Mitchell
ISBN 0 946487 15 4 PB £7.50

Of Big Hills and Wee Men
Peter Kemp
ISBN 1 84282 052 4 PB £7.99

BIOGRAPHY

Not Nebuchadnezzar: In search of identities
Jenni Calder
ISBN 1 84282 060 5 PB £9.99

The Last Lighthouse
Sharma Krauskopf
ISBN 0 946487 96 0 PB £7.99

Tobermory Teuchter
Peter Macnab
ISBN 0 946487 41 3 PB £7.99

Bare Feet & Tackety Boots
Archie Cameron
ISBN 0 946487 17 0 PB £7.95

Come Dungeons Dark
John Taylor Caldwell
ISBN 0 946487 19 7 PB £6.95

SOCIAL HISTORY

Pumpherston: the story of a shale oil village
Sybil Cavanagh
ISBN 1 84282 011 7 HB £17.99
ISBN 1 84282 015 X PB £10.99

Shale Voices
Alistair Findlay
ISBN 0 946487 78 2 HB £17.99
ISBN 0 946487 63 4 PB £10.99

A Word for Scotland
Jack Campbell
ISBN 0 946487 48 0 PB £12.99

Crofting Years
Francis Thompson
ISBN 0 946487 06 5 PB £6.95

Hall Philpstoun's Queen
Barbara and Marie Pattullo
ISBN 1 84282 095 8 PB £6.99

HISTORY

Spectacles, testicles, fags and matches: WWII RAF Commandos
Tom Atkinson
ISBN 1 84282 071 0 PB £12.99

Desire Lines: A Scottish Odyssey
David R Ross
ISBN 1 84282 033 8 PB £9.99

Scots in Canada
Jenni Calder
ISBN 1 84282 038 9 PB £7.99

Civil Warrior: extraordinary life & poems of Montrose
Robin Bell
ISBN 1 84282 013 3 HB £10.99

NATURAL WORLD

The Hydro Boys: pioneers of renewable energy
Emma Wood
ISBN 1 84282 047 8 PB £8.99

Wild Scotland
James McCarthy
photographs by Laurie Campbell
ISBN 0 946487 37 5 PB £8.99

Wild Lives: Otters – On the Swirl of the Tide
Bridget MacCaskill
ISBN 0 946487 67 7 PB £9.99

Wild Lives: Foxes – The Blood is Wild
Bridget MacCaskill
ISBN 0 946487 71 5 PB £9.99

Scotland – Land & People: An Inhabited Solitude
James McCarthy
ISBN 0 946487 57 X PB £7.99

The Highland Geology Trail
John L Roberts
ISBN 0 946487 36 7 PB £5.99

Red Sky at Night
John Barrington
ISBN 0 946487 60 X PB £8.99

Listen to the Trees
Don MacCaskill
ISBN 0 946487 65 0 PB £9.99

TRAVEL & LEISURE

Die Kleine Schottlandfibel [Scotland Guide in German]
Hans-Walter Arends
ISBN 0 946487 89 8 PB £8.99

Let's Explore Berwick-upon-Tweed
Anne Bruce English
ISBN 1 84282 029 X PB £4.99

Let's Explore Edinburgh Old Town
Anne Bruce English
ISBN 0 946487 98 7 PB £4.99

Edinburgh's Historic Mile
Duncan Priddle
ISBN 0 946487 97 9 PB £2.99

Pilgrims in the Rough: St Andrews beyond the 19th hole
Michael Tobert
ISBN 0 946487 74 X PB £7.99

SPORT

Over the Top with the Tartan Army
Andy McArthur
ISBN 0 946487 45 6 PB £7.99

Ski & Snowboard Scotland
Hilary Parke
ISBN 0 946487 35 9 PB £6.99

FICTION

Selected Stories
Dilys Rose
ISBN 1 84282 077 X PB £7.99

Lord of Illusions
Dilys Rose
ISBN 1 84282 076 1 PB £7.99

Torch
Lin Anderson
ISBN 1 84282 042 7 PB £9.99

Heartland
John MacKay
ISBN 1 84282 059 1 PB £9.99

The Blue Moon Book
Anne MacLeod
ISBN 1 84282 061 3 PB £9.99

The Glasgow Dragon
Des Dillon
ISBN 1 84282 056 7 PB £9.99

Driftnet
Lin Anderson
ISBN 1 84282 034 6 PB £9.99

The Fundamentals of New Caledonia
David Nicol
ISBN 1 84282 93 6 HB £16.99

Milk Treading
Nick Smith
ISBN 1 84282 037 0 PB £6.99

The Kitty Killer Cult
Nick Smith
ISBN 1 84282 039 7 PB £9.99

Luath Press Limited

committed to publishing well written books worth reading

LUATH PRESS takes its name from Robert Burns, whose little collie Luath (*Gael.*, swift or nimble) tripped up Jean Armour at a wedding and gave him the chance to speak to the woman who was to be his wife and the abiding love of his life. Burns called one of *The Twa Dogs* Luath after Cuchullin's hunting dog in *Ossian's Fingal.* Luath Press was established in 1981 in the heart of Burns country, and is now based a few steps up the road from Burns' first lodgings on Edinburgh's Royal Mile.
Luath offers you distinctive writing with a hint of unexpected pleasures.

Most bookshops in the UK, the US, Canada, Australia, New Zealand and parts of Europe either carry our books in stock or can order them for you. To order direct from us, please send a £sterling cheque, postal order, international money order or your credit card details (number, address of cardholder and expiry date) to us at the address below. Please add post and packing as follows: UK – £1.00 per delivery address; overseas surface mail – £2.50 per delivery address; overseas airmail – £3.50 for the first book to each delivery address, plus £1.00 for each additional book by airmail to the same address. If your order is a gift, we will happily enclose your card or message at no extra charge.

Luath Press Limited
543/2 Castlehill
The Royal Mile
Edinburgh EH1 2ND
Scotland
Telephone: 0131 225 4326 (24 hours)
Fax: 0131 225 4324
email: gavin.macdougall@luath.co.uk
Website: www.luath.co.uk